Smeller Martin

Written and illustrated by Robert Lawson

Illustrated by Robert Lawson

SMELLER MARTIN

written and illustrated by

ROBERT LAWSON, *1892 –*

New York

THE VIKING PRESS

1950

First published by The Viking Press in September 1950
Published on the same day in the Dominion of Canada
by The Macmillan Company of Canada Limited

Printed in the United States of America
By Robert Teller Sons and Dorner

To

Florence and Freddie

and

Tony March,

to

James Eades and Joe Brennan

and Old Brownie,

all of whom, without in the least suspecting it,

made this story.

R. L.

Contents

Smeller Martin

1. The Smeller

The nickname "Smeller" which his schoolmates bestowed on young Davey Martin was not intended to be in any way insulting or uncomplimentary. On the contrary, it expressed their awed admiration for his truly amazing sense of smell.

It was not until his second year at Elder Brewster Academy that Davey realized that his sense of smell was any keener than that of anyone else. He really had never thought about it much. He just took it for granted that everyone noticed all

11

the subtle, far-off odors that he did, or was as overpowered by strong, close-up odors as he was. But one day in late May it suddenly became clear that in this one respect he was quite different from his friends—in fact from almost anyone in the world.

It was late in the afternoon when his roommate Skinny Ramsey had yawningly wondered what they would have for dinner. This question always occurred to Skinny about this time of day.

Without looking up from his book Davey answered, "Irish stew."

"How do *you* know?" Skinny asked, without much interest.

"I can smell it."

And he could. The odors came from a long way off, but he could clearly distinguish the rather nondescript meat, the carrots, onions, potatoes, turnips, and even the pallid, steamy aroma of dumplings.

He named all these things and added, "There'll be chicken soup and there'll be rice pudding for dessert."

"Don't be a dope," Skinny said, rather depressed at the thought of the too frequent Irish stew. "How could anyone smell dinner from here?"

It did seem almost impossible, for the dining hall was at the extreme far end of the long tree-shaded campus, several hundred yards away, and the kitchen was back of the dining hall. Moreover, what breeze there was, was blowing away from them, straight down the campus.

"You've been mooching around the kitchen, trying to get a handout," Skinny accused. "Besides, Irish stew hasn't got much smell, or chicken soup either, and rice pudding hasn't *any*. Hasn't any taste either," he added sadly.

"No, I haven't," Davey said. "I haven't been out of the room all afternoon—been plugging on Latin." He flung the window wider open and breathed the soft air carefully. "There's pickled beets too. Can't you really smell *anything*, Skinny?"

Skinny joined him at the window and sniffed carelessly. "Of course I can't. Can't smell a darn thing—and you can't either."

He went off to wash up while Davey continued for a while to absorb and classify all the myriad delightful odors of the early evening.

At dinner, when chicken soup appeared, Skinny eyed his roommate rather reproachfully across the table. When Irish stew came on, with all the ingredients (including dumplings) that Davey had named, the look changed to one of wonder mixed with considerable rage. When the prophesied rice pudding was brought in, Skinny could no longer contain himself.

"Listen, Magic Schnozzle," he snorted, "there's something screwy about this. Either you've pulled a fast one or you ought to be in a sideshow."

In loud tones he described to the whole table how Davey had claimed the ability to smell every item of the menu the length of the campus and, by golly, had hit every one on the nose.

Of course Davey became the target of massed jeers and far from delicate witticisms. He was addressed as "The Quarter-mile Snoot," "Stink Sleuth," "Old Blindfold Test," and numerous other titles. The simplest and least offensive was "Smeller," so it was that evening that Davey became Smeller Martin, a name he was to retain throughout his life.

Back in their room Davey tried to explain to Skinny how he had always been able to smell everything and how different different things smelled, but Skinny, whose five senses were all merely normal, couldn't begin to take it in. Skinny was, by now, fairly well convinced that in this one respect his roommate was quite super-normal. He couldn't explain it and, being at the delightful age when one doesn't attempt to explain the unexplainable, was soon snoring peacefully.

Davey, however, was quite excited over it. It was a pleasant excitement too, for although he was as active and healthy as anyone, he had never been particularly outstanding in either sports or scholarship. Now he realized that this strange gift held great promise. It would set him apart from the usual run. In a quiet way he would be someone exceptional. Why, even Bus Baker, Brewster's wonder-boy halfback for whom everyone was prophesying great things at Yale, couldn't do anything like this. He might be a wizard at passing, but Davey was sure that, blindfolded, Bus couldn't *smell* the difference between a football and a canteloupe.

He lay awake for some time thinking how his whole life so

far had been mostly a succession of smells. Almost everything
that he remembered he remembered more by its smell than
by its looks. Every special occasion or happening was asso-
ciated with an odor or a combination of odors.

Such as the time he had broken his collarbone and spent
several days in the infirmary. He didn't remember much about
any pain or about what went on. What he mostly remembered
was a medley of the smells of antiseptics and disinfectants, of
medicines and gauze and plaster and adhesive tape. There
was the starchy smell of nurses' uniforms and doctors' white
coats. There was the damp smell of steam from sterilizers, the
soapy smell of scrub water, and always the turpentiney aroma
of floor wax. And the meals which broke the monotony of the
long days were never any surprise, for Davey was always
aware of their composition the moment they left the kitchen
and started up on the dumbwaiter—often before.

Even the seasons of the year were more distinguished by
their smells than by heat or cold, snow or rains. In winter
when the ground was frozen and covered with snow there
were few earth smells, so all others were far clearer. When
they went skiing or skating Davey could smell chimney
smoke a mile or more away and could tell whether the logs
were birch or oak or hickory. The warm smell of barnyards
drifted across the fields, and he could distinguish the milky
odor of cows and the strong odor of pigs and the ammonia-
like odor of horses. In the evening as they returned he could,
sometimes, as they passed a patch of woods, smell a flock of

roosting crows or a wandering dog. Once in a while he would catch the sharp scent of a fox.

As the snow began to melt in the spring and the ice on the ponds and brooks broke up, there was unleashed a perfect riot of new smells. The bare patches in the fields gave off smells of damp earth, of rotting leaves and freshly sprouted grass. The ponds and brooks fairly boiled with odors: rich bottom mud, pondweed, the varied smells of fish, turtles, frogs, and all the dozens of newly springing brookside plants. All these things and hundreds of others Davey could identify clearly. The only smell that Skinny and the others could recognize was that of skunk cabbage, and then only if a plant was bruised.

Goofer Wallace, who was a great nature nut, always claimed the discovery of the first robin, the first snake, the first woodchuck, the first violet, in fact the first of practically everything. But Davey had always *smelled* all of them long before Goofer had ever seen them.

As spring advanced the air became a great bouquet of flower odors, so many and so fragrant that it was difficult to pick out the different ones.

Summer had its own smell. The riot of flowers was now drowned in the rich aroma of things ripening. Vegetables, hay, grains, fruits, all gave off a heavy winy smell. Even passing bees, laden with honey and pollen, smelled heavily sweet.

Then came autumn, and the smell of ripe apples and

grapes almost blotted out everything else. Almost, but not quite, for Davey. He could sense a different smell to the stubbled hay fields, the over-lush grass of the campus lawns. He could smell clearly, though faintly, ripe pumpkins dotting the fields, the dry dusty odor of shocked corn.

After the first killing frost and autumn rains there was another complete smell-change. All odors became dank and sour. The ivy on the buildings, the matted grass, the rotting leaves, the neglected gardens—all gave off the rank smell of death and decay—the death of another year.

But now it was May and the spring smells were at their most glorious. Davey tiptoed to the window and looked out over the misty campus. He sniffed gently. He could tell that the daffodils over by the woods were about gone—their smell was a bit sour. The lilacs were at their best, most of the other flowering shrubs were in bloom. Only a few tulips were out yet but the others were coming along; he could smell the freshness of their new leaves and of the iris blades. There were dozens of other delicious odors, each clear and distinct.

A car passed the corner of the campus. Yes, that would be Professor McIlhenny's old Buick. It always leaked oil and he could recognize the smoky exhaust. And from down the length of the whole campus, far off, but to him perfectly distinct, came the faint odor of steeping prunes. Skinny had had a faint hope that they might have oranges for breakfast, but they wouldn't. It would be prunes again.

This newly discovered gift of Davey's promised to afford him and Skinny not only a good deal of amusement and interest but considerable profit as well. A day or so later Skinny came into their room after an afternoon spent in various pursuits.

"Well," greeted Davey without looking up, "what were you doing catching? Thought you thought you were a pitcher."

"What makes you think I was playing ball?" Skinny demanded. "And how'd you know I was catching?"

"Smelled the glove on your hand," Davey yawned. "And what's more, it was a catcher's mitt. They smell entirely different from the other gloves."

"But I had a shower," Skinny protested, eying his left hand in some amazement, "and a swim in the pool."

"Yes, I know. I can smell the pool water on your hair and the locker room on your clothes. Those lockers stink—I can smell them from here."

Skinny sat a moment in deep thought, then a bright light seemed to dawn. "S-a-a-y," he exclaimed happily, "there's money in this, boy. You just do your nose stuff and leave the management to good old Ramsey. We'll clean up a million— or a couple of bucks anyway."

Shortly thereafter Doc Whitcomb lounged in at the door.

"Doc," Skinny challenged, "I've got a dime says Smeller can tell just what you've been doing all afternoon."

Doc produced two nickels. "These say he can't."

"You, my boy," pronounced Davey, after a careless sniff, "have been messing around in the lab all afternoon. Using mostly—let's see—nitric acid, sulphuric acid, carbon, sulphur, sodium, and a lot of that junk. You washed your hands with that nasty green soap, but it didn't do much good. Also, on your way back you stopped at Billy's and bought some sort of a mucky candy bar and ate it. I can't exactly identify it because they're all alike."

"Racketeers," Doc grunted, throwing down his two nickels. He departed, but returned to stick his head in the door and add, "Confidence men, ghouls, yeggs!"

The next client was Goofer Wallace, the nature enthusiast. Goofer was always well heeled in the way of spending money and Skinny greeted his appearance with enthusiasm.

"Goofer, old man," he hailed, "here is your chance of a lifetime to make—or lose—one complete quarter of a dollar. Our friend Smeller guarantees to tell, by nose alone, exactly what you've been doing this afternoon. We are glad to wager twenty-five cents, one quarter of a dollar, that he can."

Goofer confidently laid a half-dollar on the table. "All right, I'll double you. He can't."

Davey leaned back in his chair and, adopting a judicial air, pronounced, "Young Mr. Wallace has spent all the afternoon rambling in the woods. He poked some at a woodchuck's hole and stirred around in the brook looking for frogs' eggs— any nose would know that. But mostly he robbed the nests of poor helpless little songbirds. His clothes reek of bark and

sap and pine resin and his hands of birds' nests. He collected
a great many eggs and blew them out. The pretty shells,
which are now in his pocket, smell to heaven."

Goofer rather dazedly extracted a handful of neatly blown
birds' eggs from his coat pocket, gazed sadly at them and his
half-dollar and left without protest.

"Pal," gloated Skinny, collecting the loot, "we're in the big
money now. Let's us make hay while the sun shines."

The sun shone on their racket for longer than it should, for
all the victims were too sheepish to broadcast their fleecing.
By the time the entire Second Class had been well exploited,
the community chest of Ramsey, Martin & Co. contained the
handsome sum of nine dollars and eighty-five cents.

It might have led to some slight ill feeling had not Davey,
coming down the corridor one evening after dinner, suddenly
been electrified by the delicious odor of chocolate cake. It
took only a sniff or two to locate the source—Pod Smith's
room. It *would* be his room, for Pod was a notorious pig, and
his door *would* be locked, naturally. He had had a package
from home that morning.

It took only a few minutes to collect a ravenous group—
dessert that night had been the usual rice pudding. All of
them had been victims of the Skinny-Smeller racket and all
were still slightly suspicious.

"Men," Skinny announced pleasantly, "just to prove that
this firm is honest, aboveboard, and not entirely interested
in money-making, who's for some chocolate cake, entirely for

free? A cake located by the marvelous nose of the great Smeller Martin."

There was a hungry growl.

Skinny stepped down the corridor and rapped officiously on Pod Smith's door. "Special delivery letter for you, Pod," he called. "Looks important. May be a check."

The door was opened only a crack, but the crack was immediately widened to full by eight or ten eager shoulders. Luckily the owner had managed to consume only about a fourth of the cake, so the remainder, when divided into fairly equal portions, gave a most generous slice to each and every one—except Pod Smith.

Had the Class Prophecy been written that evening, Smeller Martin certainly would have been listed as "Most Popular" and Skinny Ramsey as "Most Likely to Succeed."

2. Lavender Hill

It was fun to be home again with three whole months of vacation lying ahead. Of course Davey did miss Skinny Ramsey and the rest for a few days, but what was that compared to the joy of no classes, of lying in bed as long as you pleased mornings, and the super-joy of Rose's food? Three months with never the threat of Irish stew or rice pudding!

Davey's father being one of the country's most prominent playwrights, and his mother being perhaps its most popular and beloved actress, they were away a great deal. In fact Davey could almost count on his fingers the few times his parents had ever been at home.

These visits were always wonderful and exciting. There were always fabulous presents, brought him from New York or London or Paris. There were guests coming and going, packages and telegrams arriving, the telephone ringing incessantly. Rose would have her nephew and niece to help in the kitchen. McKinley, who usually tended the grounds, became butler.

Both Mother and Father would relax and say how marvelously peaceful it was to be living in the country again. "By George," his father always said, "this is *really* living. We *must* settle down soon, Garda, and get some pleasure out of life. This squirrel-cage existence we carry on is preposterous. Just as soon as this next play is settled . . ." Mother would smile her wonderful smile and agree with him.

Then, always, within a few days, there would be a visit from some highly important producer or a long-distance telephone call from New York or Hollywood or London. There would be a mad scramble of packing, hasty tearful farewells. Then a great quiet would settle over the place.

Rose's niece and nephew would depart, McKinley would go back to his gardening. Davey and Aunt Agatha would resume their quiet life together. The only reminders of his parents would be the fading odors of Father's cigar smoke and Mother's exotic perfumes and powders.

But Aunt Agatha was always there, she always had been, as long as Davey could remember.

When Davey was born his mother had insisted that they buy this country place. "Davey is going to have a normal life," she had said firmly. "He's not going to be dragged around from pillar to post like most theater children, and he's not going to be shunted off on schools and camps and governesses. Besides, when we can settle down this will be a real place to settle." When it soon became apparent that they never would settle down, Father's sister Agatha came to take over, and remained, becoming more of a mother to Davey, really, than his own mother.

Aunt Agatha was a tiny, charming, birdlike person. Her clothes, in fact she and all her possessions, were crisp and dainty and smelled of lavender. She walked always in a pleasant aura of lavender: lavender soap, lavender sachet, lavender dusting powder, lavender perfume. Davey, with his sensitive nose, could always tell where she was; in her room, in the living room, on the terrace, or in the garden.

As a matter of fact, it was this fondness for lavender which had given the place its name. When the question of a name for the new house had first come up John Martin had said, "Well, it's on a hill and always reeks of lavender. What, therefore, more appropriate than Lavender Hill?" So Lavender Hill it became.

Aunt Agatha was always pleasantly busy, overseeing the household and the garden, cutting and arranging flowers, putting things away in mothballs and taking things out of mothballs, darning or sewing on buttons for Davey.

In Davey's eyes she had only two weaknesses, and these were both very slight ones. One was her preoccupation with church work and the Reverend Otis Beasley.

The Reverend Beasley, a middle-aged widower, came to tea about once a week. He seemed a rather colorless person, but Aunt Agatha said he was a fine character and a most earnest worker. Davey never thought much about him one way or the other. He would probably have liked him better if the Reverend had not insisted on being a regular fellow. He was everlastingly slapping Davey on the shoulder and asking about his school and his studies. If there was anything Davey didn't want to think about or talk about during vacation, it was school.

Aunt Agatha's other failing was a deep concern with the Walls of the Stomach. Many years before she had read a book by a prominent physician who believed that practically all human ills were caused by the action of wrong foods, drinks, nerves, and overwork on the lining of the stomach. The book was called *The Walls of Health,* and for some unknown reason Aunt Agatha had taken it seriously. Perhaps it was because she had met the author at a reception and he had autographed her copy of the book.

At any rate, she always considered carefully what effect

anything she or anyone else ate might have on the walls of the stomach. Often when Davey was helping himself to a third portion of dessert she would gently chide, "Remember, darling, the walls—*the walls.*" But Davey never bothered much.

She even tried to make a convert of Rose, with still less success. "Lawd, Miss Agtha," Rose chuckled, "my stummick's got no walls; it's only got a top and a bottom. When it's empty I notice the bottom, and when it's full I'm conscious of the top. Otherwise me and my stummick gets on fine."

But the Reverend Beasley listened with great sympathy and attention. He even borrowed the book and read it, and thereafter regulated his diet strictly according to its teachings.

Although Aunt Agatha was only in her middle thirties she seemed, of course, to one of Davey's age, quite an ancient spinster. It came as a real shock to him when Rose hinted that the Reverend would not be at all opposed to making Miss Agatha his bride. To Davey the thought of the Reverend Beasley making *anyone* his bride seemed strange, but Aunt Agatha! It was unthinkable. He tried to laugh it off.

"You needn't to laugh," Rose pointed out. "You never can tell. 'Tain't as though she was *old.* 'Course she ain't too young neither, but thirty-four's a nice marriageable age. She certainly is a sweet pretty lady, and what's moreover she got a ton or two of money. Ain't anybody goin' to object to that, 'specially a Reverent."

This was an angle that had never occurred to Davey.

While Rose was devoted to Miss Agatha, her greatest object of adoration was Davey's mother. When Garda Garrison's first meteoric success burst upon the world Rose had been her maid, dresser, confidante, adviser, and constant companion. Several times they had crossed the ocean and traversed the continent together. Rose's social standing rose to dizzy heights. She was personal maid to Garda Garrison!

She would still have been, had it not been for the advent of airplane travel. After Garda's marriage to John Martin their numerous engagements made plane travel a necessity, and at this point Rose rebelled. "No'm, Miss Garda," she announced firmly. "Boats and trains—yes; but them things—*no*. Not for me, never. I'm staying on the ground all in one piece."

So on the ground she stayed. When Davey arrived and the country place had been purchased, Rose revealed that she was an even better cook than maid and settled down to country life with great contentment. She often regaled Davey or McKinley with accounts of "our" triumphs in New York, London, Chicago, or Hollywood, but never with any great regret for these lost glories.

McKinley, the last member of the household, was not strictly of it, for he went home nights to a wife and four or five children. But every morning, promptly at eight, his battered Ford would struggle up the drive and park under the big maple tree. A few moments later the clatter of the lawnmower or the click of his clippers would hail the new day.

Six feet two and built with the powerful grace of a panther, McKinley had the heart and spirit of an exceptionally sweet child. His gentle voice had the mellow depth of organ notes and the same soothing effect. Miss Agatha often said that whenever she heard McKinley laugh she always knew that the world could not be nearly as sorry a place as the radio commentators claimed.

Davey and McKinley were constant companions. Davey loved him almost as much as he did Aunt Agatha or Rose. The only slight trouble that resulted from this companionship was caused by their mutual love of fires. Whenever the fire siren in the village sounded its alarm, both Davey and McKinley, no matter what the importance of their occupations, streaked for the big maple tree. A moment later the old Ford would careen madly down the drive. Their return, sometimes hours later, usually found some tasks uncompleted; the terrace perhaps unswept, or the roses half cultivated.

If taxed with these delinquencies McKinley would merely smile his disarming smile and chuckle, "Sorry, Miss Agtha, but when that old sireen hoot Mist' Davey and me we just *got* to go."

Although she felt it her duty to protest, Aunt Agatha could understand. She had often felt tempted to join them herself. After all, thirty-four wasn't so terribly old.

3. "My Own Letters in Gold"

After dinner, that first night at home, Aunt Agatha brought Davey up to date on all the local news.

McKinley's wife had had a new baby, either the fifth or sixth, she couldn't remember. It was a boy and had been named Ulysses David Calhoun Williams. "You must remember to congratulate him, dear, because he'll never bother to mention it to you," Aunt Agatha reminded. "Although," she added, "I really think that after the fifth or sixth, congratulations are hardly in order."

There had been a long letter from Mother in London yesterday. "Yes," Davey said. "I smelled it when I passed your desk. Doesn't Mother use the darnedest perfumes?"

"They are given to her," Aunt Agatha explained. "All the famous perfumers fight for the privilege. They are supposed to add glamour, though what further glamour could possibly be added to dear Garda I can't imagine.

"The new play, of course, is a huge success. She sent a large batch of reviews, all quite ecstatic. It will have a long run. Heaven knows when they will be able to come home.

"They sent Rose a beautiful silk scarf and McKinley a pigskin wallet. There is a package for you—I think a field glass—and of course John sent me the usual wristwatch. Poor John! Every big success inspires him to send me a handsome wristwatch. This I believe is the eighth, and I've *never* worn a wristwatch.

"The Reverend Beasley came for tea yesterday—"

"Yes, I smelled him," Davey said.

"*Darling!* What a thing to say," Aunt Agatha gasped. "Of course I know that your sense of smell is unusually keen. But the Reverend Beasley!"

"Oh, it isn't *bad* especially," Davey said. "Not a real stench —just the usual stuff. You know, dusty carpets and stuffy cushions, prayer books and incense, and mice."

Aunt Agatha hastily changed the subject. "We have a new

neighbor, a Professor Benton. Really an ex-professor, he is retired, at quite an early age. I have always thought of retired professors as old, old gentlemen with long white beards, but Professor Benton is not at all like that. In his forties, I would think, and most charming. I have met him once or twice. He once taught at Brewster, so I told him about you. He said he would be delighted to meet you. I really think you might go over and call on him."

The idea of calling on a professor, even a retired one, did not rouse much enthusiasm in Davey, but he politely inquired where the Professor lived.

"He bought the Barker place, just over the hill. I understand he has done wonders with the old house and garden. I would really like to know."

"All right, I'll go over and snoop for you some time," Davey said, laughing. "Is he married?"

Aunt Agatha flushed, just a trace. "No, he is a bachelor. He has a couple who look after him, but not too well, I'm afraid. He had a dreadful tobacco burn on his coat and a missing shirt button.

"And Bert is coming day after tomorrow to cut the hay," Aunt Agatha wound up her budget of news.

"Oh, good," Davey said. "That's always fun. How is Bert?"

"Just as miserable and shiftless as usual." Aunt Agatha sighed. "And his adored Sonny Boy has now become old enough to engage the attention of the police occasionally. They are a sad lot, the Carters."

Davey kissed his aunt and started up to bed. "Your roses are doing fine," he said.

"But, Davey, you haven't even seen the garden yet!"

"I can smell them." He laughed. "They smell good and healthy."

The package did contain a field glass, a wonderful one, tremendously powerful and, he judged, frightfully expensive. The carrying case and strap were of beautifully stitched, rich-smelling English leather. He hung it on the back of a chair where he could enjoy the pungent aroma. It was the last thing he smelled before going to sleep and the first on waking in the morning.

McKinley greeted Davey with deep though quiet pleasure. During the day he gradually unfolded *his* packet of news and doings. There were three new woodchuck burrows in the south field. There was a family of skunks in the thicket beyond the stone wall. He had had trouble with a deer that had invaded the vegetable garden several times. He had shot five bothersome crows and had saved their bills for Davey. They had been rubbed until they looked like polished ebony. "Don't know's they any real *use* to you," he said, presenting them, "but they do *look* real pretty."

There had not been much in the way of fires, only a few grass fires and a couple of chickencoops. The one really worthwhile one had been a cleaning establishment in the village. "That one started out real rampagerous," McKinley recalled, "but it was too near the firehouse. That old Vigilant Number One got there almost as soon as I did. They got three hoses on it and woosh! Might' nigh blew that little old shack into the river."

He admired Davey's new field glass extravagantly but didn't care to look through it. "Shore is mighty handsome, but I never could *see* through them things. My eyes pretty good anyway."

Davey knew that McKinley had the eyesight of a hawk, but he himself had a wonderful time with the new glass. Birds in distant trees seemed only an arm's length away. He could see people clear across the valley working in gardens, driving cars, playing tennis. He even got a look at the new skunk family, seemingly so close that it was quite startling.

McKinley washed his hands at the tap, carefully dried them, and called Davey over to the old Ford. From the glove compartment he drew a small flat package wrapped in newspaper. He untied the string, unrolled several layers of newspaper and then of tissue paper, and at last revealed the beautiful pigskin wallet. He lovingly stroked its smooth surface, inhaled deeply its rich leathery aroma. "Ain't that an elegant scent?" he sighed. "Smells real much like that case to your spyglass."

He proudly pointed out to Davey the monogram, stamped in gold leaf. "McK.W.," he read softly. "McKinley Williams. Mist' Davey, this is the first thing in all my life ever I owned had my own letters printed on it, McK.W. And it come all the way from London, England!" He wrapped it again, almost reverently, tied the string, and replaced the package in the glove compartment.

"I keep it in there," he said, smiling, " 'cause ain't no place in the house those chillen ain't into. 'Course I only aim to use it on Sundays. But when I pull it out in church and take out my contribution to drop in the plate, that old congregation's goin' to see *something*."

McKinley also commented on the new neighbor, Professor Benton. "Seem like a real nice gent'man," he said. "Tell you what he done was *real* nice. Last week, day after the new young 'un was born, I was up on top the hill there pullin' up poison ivry 'long the stone wall. This gent'man he come walkin' round on his field and he stop and talk with me real pleasant. Somehow I come to tell him about young Ulysses David Calhoun, and he stick out his hand and say, 'What about the seegar? I always heard proud fathers hand out seegars.'

"I laugh and tell him after five of 'em, proud fathers don't *have* no seegars. Well, he laugh too and walk away, but 'bout an hour later he come strollin' up again with a great big ol' box of elegant long seegars under his arm. 'Here,' he say, and hand 'em to me, 'now you can do it right,' he say.

"I gave him a seegar and he stuck it in his pocket and then he shake hands with me and say, 'My best regards to Ulysses David Calhoun,' he say. 'Bring him up proper,' he say. 'See that he always tells the truth and votes the straight Republican ticket.'

"They much too fine to give away, but I certainly am enjoying them," McKinley finished happily. "Come Sunday when I walk down to church, smokin' one of those elegant long seegars and with that rich-smellin' wallet in my pocket, I sho' will be walkin' in Zion."

4. The Carter Tribe

Before he was up the next morning Davey could hear the popping of a tractor, the rattle of mower blades, and the raucous voices of the Carter tribe. By the time he had finished breakfast and gone out, almost half of the south hayfield had been cut.

The Carters greeted him according to their various ways, Bert with loud jollity and Uncle Eppa with his senile cackle.

Sonny Boy, who was driving the tractor, waved with a studied nonchalance that verged on indifference.

Bert was short and fat, with a round red face which bore a striking resemblance to a Santa Claus without whiskers. Despite a lifetime of failures he was always loudly cheerful and incurably optimistic. The tail end of an old family which had been steadily degenerating since Colonial days, he had, some years before, inherited a fine old house and a hundred acres or more of the best farm land in the district. He had promptly built a huge dairy barn, which he couldn't pay for, and acquired a herd of cows, which he couldn't care for. The fine old house soon bulged with children, relatives, and in-laws. He sold the paneling and mantels from the house to interior decorators and all the topsoil from the rich acres to contractors. This left little pasturage and no hay for the cows, so he was reduced to collecting hay from all those places in the countryside whose owners were willing to put up with his noise and sloppy methods.

Bert, as the neighbors aptly put it, was "always up to the neck in debts and cow manure."

For some unaccountable reason he worshiped his grandson Sonny Boy, whose actual name was Clyde. In Bert's eyes Sonny Boy could do no wrong. In the eyes of their neighbors, and recently of the police, he could do little else.

Before Davey went away to school he and Sonny Boy had been close friends. They had gone fishing and swimming and skating and had hunted woodchucks together. In spite of some reservations Davey had always rather liked him. But now Sonny Boy had suddenly grown up. He was fifteen and Davey only twelve. Sonny Boy had developed a cheap sophistication and a loud contempt for any kid of twelve.

Bert's eyes followed Sonny Boy with adoration as he rode the bouncing tractor. Sonny Boy always disdained a shirt while working, his skinny torso was well browned and lately decorated with a tattooed eagle and an American flag. He wore a Sears Roebuck sombrero and a broad belt set with glass reflector buttons, stolen from highway signs.

"Look at the way he handles that tractor," gloated Bert in maudlin admiration. "Smart as a whip, that young jigger is. Goin' places he is."

"Goin' to hell, that's where," Uncle Eppa cackled. "Goin' to jail in a jalopy, that's where he's goin'."

"You know, Davey," Bert continued proudly, "that young squirt's got himself a car. Yessir, an old Ford. Cut her down and souped her up all himself. Painted her bright blue with orange wheels. Got a muffler cutout and a horn that plays 'How Dry I Am.' She can make eighty miles an hour easy. Been arrested twice and outrun the cops three times. He's a smart lad, none smarter.

"Great reader too; got a stack of them comic books tall as you are. He can read off one of them in half an hour. Smarter than them dumb teachers of his. Waste of time, his goin' to school any more, so we let him quit."

"Readin' himself into trouble, that's what," Uncle Eppa

croaked. "Too much education, that's what. Crazy as a coot. All the young ones is crazy. Ain't like in my time."

Davey had never quite known whose uncle Uncle Eppa was. He was just one of the sprawling Carter household. In youth he had been kicked on the head by a horse, and the deep semicircular indentation on his forehead had always fascinated Davey. It made one eye droop, but the other was bright as a blue jay's wing. This ancient injury brought on occasional headaches, and Uncle Eppa's trusted cure for these was a mixture of warm beer and cheap red wine, a jug of which he always carried in the truck. This nauseating mixture brought on even worse headaches, so Uncle Eppa's life was a vicious cycle of headaches. The only thing that he was really sure of was that most of the world was crazy. He could, however, build a good load of hay and he got on well with the cows.

He could drive the tractor well enough to rake and now prepared to do so while Sonny Boy sprawled in the shade. "That's right, Sonny Boy, take yourself some rest," Bert called. "Looks like rain and we may have to hustle later on."

Davey sniffed the air carefully. "It isn't going to rain," he announced. "I can always smell it coming and I don't smell any now."

Uncle Eppa burst into a spasm of cackles and Sonny Boy guffawed derisively. "Listen to the wise guy," he jeered. "Smell the rain! Where'd you learn that one—at that fancy-pants school they send you to? Smell rain comin'—of all the dopes!"

"Hope you're right, Davey boy, hope you're right," Bert laughed as he started to cock up hay.

Davey brought his new field glass to show to Sonny Boy. Sonny Boy snatched it eagerly and began to peer at the surrounding countryside. "Boy!" he breathed, "ain't *that* a glass!" He examined all its details, and Davey was startled by the covetous gleam that, for a moment, swept his face. "Bet that set your old man back a wad of money. What's a glass like that worth, a hundred bucks—maybe two hundred?"

"I haven't any idea," Davey said, "I guess good glasses are pretty expensive."

"I'll say. Made in England too." Sonny Boy had resumed his peering. "Oh, boy," he gloated, "I can see a gal playing tennis clear over on the Easton Road. Wearin' shorts too, and I *mean* short."

He reluctantly handed the glass back to Davey and his eyes took on a hard look. "Must be soft to have an old man that can send you presents like that."

"I guess I *am* pretty lucky," Davey said, hanging the glass on a tree branch. "Father sent McKinley a wallet too. It's a beautiful pigskin one with his initials on it." He laughed. "McKinley keeps it in his car because he thinks it's too grand to use."

"Well, what do you know!" Sonny Boy spat disgustedly. "He certainly must have plenty of dough to throw around." His hard eyes fastened on McKinley, who was leisurely hoeing the vegetable garden. His thin lips twisted venomously.

"Sending a wallet all the way from London to *him*. Look at him—getting paid good money for leaning on his hoe and us sweating our heads off for a couple of lousy loads of hay."

"McKinley's all right," Davey protested, wondering somewhat.

"All right if you like him," Sonny Boy snarled. He snatched up his fork and angrily went to work.

It was midafternoon before they began to load. The sky looked more threatening than ever, but still Davey smelled no rain coming. Uncle Eppa was on the truck, and Davey, Bert, and Sonny Boy pitched up to him.

"Ain't going to try to make it in one load, are you?" Sonny Boy asked.

"Think we'd better," Bert answered, glancing anxiously at the scudding black clouds. "Don't want to leave half a load to get wet—hay's scarce."

"It isn't going to rain," Davey said.

"Aw, you and your smeller," Sonny Boy grunted. "You're nuts!"

"All nuts," Uncle Eppa cackled. "Crazy as bedbugs. Toss it up, boys, toss it up! I'll build you a load high as a house. Build it high as the moon. Come on, toss it up, toss it up!"

He did build a magnificent load, square cornered and solid but ridiculously high. The cab of the truck was completely buried. Still Bert continued to pile on more hay. The sky was so dark now that it seemed almost twilight. A wind had sprung up and the leaves of the tossing maples showed their lighter undersides. It certainly looked like the moment before a downpour, but still Davey smelled no rain.

Finally Bert said, "That'll do. Run get your things, Sonny Boy, and let's go."

"Let's go," Uncle Eppa screeched. "Take 'er away! I've built 'er and she'll stand. Drive 'er away, Crazy Boy! Drive 'er away!"

Sonny Boy raced down the hill, carrying the extra forks, his shirt and sombrero. He wormed his way into the cab, and the huge load started down toward the gate, swaying perilously.

"Take it easy! Take it easy!" shrieked Uncle Eppa, perched atop the load, but Sonny Boy was driving recklessly. Near the gate where the road was rutted the truck pitched and yawed. Then, quite slowly, it turned over on its side. Two thirds of the load, plus Uncle Eppa cackling curses, slid off in a disorderly welter.

Fortunately they had a rope, and with this and the aid of the tractor the truck was righted, with about one third of its original load.

"Well," Bert said sadly, "half a loaf is better than none."

"Come on," Sonny Boy snarled, releasing the brakes, "let's get going." They went off down the road, strewing hay at every turn.

McKinley, about to leave, stood looking over the messy field. "My goodness," he chuckled, "if there's a wrong way to do anything that Mr. Bert he sure can find it."

Davey agreed. "They needn't have hurried so," he said. "I told them it wasn't going to rain."

"Course it ain't," McKinley said, glancing toward the west. Already the clouds had broken, showing brilliant patches of green-blue sky. It had not rained a drop.

Davey hastened up to the house to take a shower. He was hot and sweaty and covered with hayseed and the dinner hour was approaching. It was not until after dinner that he remembered the field glass hung on the tree branch and went out to get it.

It wasn't there.

At first he thought that McKinley might have taken it in, but surely he would have mentioned it. Then he thought he might have the wrong tree, but he sniffed the branch and the smell of the leather strap was perfectly clear, he couldn't be mistaken.

Slowly a chilling feeling of depression settled on him. He remembered that queer covetous look that had flashed over Sonny Boy's face as he fingered the glass. He remembered the hard look in his eyes as he spoke of its value. He remembered Sonny Boy racing up the hill to get his shirt and sombrero.

Still he couldn't believe it. Of course you read in the papers and heard on the radio of people actually stealing things— cars, money, jewelry, silver. But those were vague, far-off people, professionals many of them. They weren't anyone you had known for years, had played with and fished with and gone swimming with. People you knew that well *couldn't* do a thing like that. Yet the vague chilling suspicion settled more heavily.

He didn't mention it to Aunt Agatha—he couldn't yet. They played a few games of Chinese checkers, but his mind was not on the game.

"You're tired, darling," she said. "You shouldn't have pitched all that hay so soon after lunch. Violent exercise too soon after eating has a very bad effect on the walls of the stomach." He kissed her and went up to bed, but in spite of his tiredness he didn't sleep very well.

5. Good Friends and Bad

Next morning Davey waked to loud talk, shouts, and cackles. From his bedroom window he could see Bert and Uncle Eppa loading the spilled hay from yesterday's fiasco. Sonny Boy was not present.

Somehow he did not care to face any of the Carter clan this morning and was glad to accompany Aunt Agatha to the village. Aunt Agatha had to see about the floral decorations at the church and do some other errands. She parked the car at Old Trinity, and Davey wandered about town.

He had his hair cut, went to the library and drew out a couple of books, bought some magazines, and window-shopped at all the hardware stores. He got a package of cigarettes for McKinley and a small box of peppermints for Rose. He met and passed the time of day with many old friends: Otto Abel, the butcher, Herman Smith, the garbage man, Mr. Sniffen, the president of the bank, and various others.

It was a pleasant morning. By the time he rejoined Aunt Agatha the problem of the missing field glass did not seem so depressing. After all, there might be another explanation. Perhaps Aunt Agatha or Rose had taken it in and had kept silent, just to teach him not to be so careless. A wandering dog might even have pulled it down and dragged it away somewhere. Someone *could* have come in and taken it while they were at dinner. By the time lunch was over he felt quite up to seeing the Carters. Sonny Boy was out in the field, driving the tractor, raking. He greeted Davey with a condescending wave, just as usual. Bert was noisily cheerful.

"Well, Davey boy," he bellowed, "you sure did smell it right yesterday. Never rained a drop. Got in the rest of the load this morning and we'll clean up this field this afternoon easy. You certainly can't smell any rain today." He laughed, looking up at the crisp blue sky. It really did seem a well-nigh perfect haying day.

"But I *do*," Davey answered, smelling the air thoughtfully. "You'd better get along with it—it's going to rain hard. I can smell it awfully strong."

"Now, Davey boy, don't try to kid old Bert."

"Who ever seen rain on a day like this?" Sonny Boy jeered. "You're crazy, you and your schnozzle. Whyn't you give it a good blow?"

"Ain't crazy as the rest of you," cackled Uncle Eppa. "I knowed a lady could smell water. Every time a man was set to dig a well she'd go all over the place on her hands and knees, snuffin' like a hound dog. Then she'd rise up and stomp her foot on the ground and yell, 'Dig here.' And they'd dig there, and by gum they'd find water every time."

"Can always find water if you dig long enough," Bert bawled.

"Dig deep enough and you might find beer and red wine," jeered Sonny Boy.

The Carter clan seemed exactly as usual. Davey could note not the slightest sign of uneasy conscience in Sonny Boy's manner. There *must* be some other explanation. His spirits lightened and he decided to pitch some hay.

There was an extra fork stuck in the ground, and Sonny Boy's shirt was hanging on it. Davey picked the shirt off to hang on a bush and then, like a blow in the pit of the stomach, it struck him—the clean sharp smell of English leather. He sniffed the shirt thoroughly. Just as clearly as though a stripe had been painted on it he could trace the course of the shoulder strap, over the left shoulder, down and across the front and back. He hung the shirt back on the fork and started back toward the house. He felt a little sick.

"Ain't you goin' to help us before that flood comes?" Bert guffawed. Davey didn't answer him.

He sought out McKinley. Talking with him was always soothing. He found him in the pine wood up on top of the hill. McKinley did not care for the Carters and when they were present always found something to do as far away as possible. Now he was cutting up dead pine branches and uprooting sumac.

"How those mens gettin' along with their hay, Mist' Davey?" he asked.

"Oh, all right," Davey answered. "They ought to hurry though. I told them I smelled rain, but they just laughed at me."

McKinley straightened up and let the pleasant breeze blow on his face, sampling it. "Sho is," he agreed. "Hard rain too. Reckon they'll let it get wet and be noisin' aroun' here another day or two. Wish they'd finish up and clar out. I don't like 'em messin' aroun' our place somehow."

Davey felt much the same—now. "McKinley," he asked, "can you really smell rain coming the way I can?"

McKinley smiled. "Well, now, I can't exactly say do I *smell* it; more like I just seem to *feel* it, and I sho do feel it now."

He went back to his wood cutting and Davey piled the cut pieces in neat ranks. Suddenly the pine wood became dark and still. They went to the edge of the grove and looked out over the valley. To the north and west a heavy bank of black clouds was boiling up. Already it had blotted out the sun and was advancing rapidly.

"Yon she come." McKinley laughed. "Now maybe them Carter mens goin' to believe you when you tell 'em somethin'." He gathered up the tools leisurely; they still had a few minutes. From the louder bawling and increased racket they knew that the Carters were at last making speed. As they walked down the hillside they could see Bert and Sonny Boy frantically pitching up the last few cocks.

"My goodness," said McKinley, "a man could feed two cows for a year on what they spills."

The rain swept in before they had reached the tool house and they sprinted for its shelter. Through the streaming windows they watched the truck lumbering toward the field gate, Uncle Eppa perched on top, screaming like a banshee. It wasn't a very big load, and they should have had it in the barn by now.

"Goin' to be mighty wet hay, time they get home," McKinley said, chuckling. "Mighty wet old man too. Well, leas'-wise they thu an' gone. I'll clean up their leavin's tomorrow and put that ol' chain back on the gate. Then maybe we'll have some peacefulness 'round here again."

The rain drummed like thunder on the roof. Davey settled on a bag of hayseed and McKinley puttered around, sweeping the floor and hanging up tools.

"You enjoying your spyglass, Mist' Davey?" he asked.

Davey had almost forgotten, for a moment. The question brought the sick-feeling depression. "Yes," he answered, "it's fine."

"I certainly am lookin' forward to Sunday," McKinley said, leaning on his broom, his face lit with happy anticipation. "I've been thinkin' and sort of plannin'. I'll be settin' up there near the front of the church with two-three of them elegant long seegars stickin' out my breas' pocket, all wrapped in cellofame. Think I'll sit in an aisle seat. Then when Deacon Eades come along with the collection plate I'll reach in and draw out my grand wallet, real slow and dignified. I'll open 'er up wide and hold 'er open so folks can see my letters, my gol' letters, McK.W. Then maybe I'll clear my thoat a little, like this—'Ahem.' I'll take out my contribution and put it in the plate, easy like. Then maybe I'll take a li'l smell of that rich smellin' leather and I'll fold 'er up and put 'er back in my inside pocket, just like a banker er a lawer er somebody. Goin' to wear that elegant dark blue coat your daddy give me last summer. Figurin' to press it tonight."

The rain continued to pour, so they draped themselves in a couple of sacks and ran, McKinley to his old Ford and Davey to the house.

6. "She's Gone!"

Davey woke next morning with a vague feeling of depression, which, at first, he couldn't account for. It certainly was a fine fresh morning. A gentle breeze stirred the curtains and brought all sorts of thrilling summer scents. Then he caught the faint pungent odor of leather from the chairback where he had hung his field glass—and it all came back to him.

He lay awhile, wondering what he ought to do. He was

virtually certain now that Sonny Boy had stolen the glass—
that leather smell on the shirt was too clear to leave any doubt.
Yet he had no proof except that one whiff, and no one would
take *that* seriously.

He couldn't tell Aunt Agatha; she would insist on reporting
it to the police. He could imagine the hearty laugh *they*
would have if he told them about smelling leather on someone's shirt. Besides, Sonny Boy by now would have it well
hidden or, more likely, sold.

He went down to breakfast in a gloomy mood, only to find
still greater gloom in the breakfast room. Aunt Agatha was
slightly red-eyed and silent. Rose's usually beaming countenance was grim and set.

"Well," Davey said with forced cheerfulness, "everyone
seems pretty low. What's the matter? Bad news?" Rose went
out to the kitchen.

"Yes, dear," Aunt Agatha answered, "I will tell you about
it *after* you have eaten *and* digested your breakfast. Nothing
has so bad an effect on the walls of the stomach, you know,
as eating when mentally disturbed."

"Nothing about Dad or Mother?" Davey asked hastily.

"No, no, darling, nothing like that." She rose and kissed
him and went out.

Rose brought his breakfast in somber silence. "For Pete's
sake, what's going on?" Davey demanded. "You're all cheerful
as a funeral."

"You'll find out," Rose answered. "Now eat your breakfast,

like Miss Agtha tell you, and mind them walls." She attempted a smile, but it didn't amount to much.

Davey finished his breakfast and sought out McKinley. Perhaps *he* could explain this gloom. He found him in the vegetable garden, cultivating. McKinley looked up at his cheery greeting, and Davey was startled by the look on his stricken face. He replied, but there were no twinkling eyes, no gentle smile.

McKinley looked above Davey's head, his dull eyes fixed on the far horizon. "Mist' Davey," he said, "she's gone."

"Who?" Davey asked stupidly.

"My beautiful wallet. My wallet come all the way from London, England. My elegant wallet with my own letters on it in gold. She's gone."

"Gone? Stolen?" Davey gasped. Aunt Agatha certainly was right about the Walls. He could feel them growing chill, contracting. "Why, McKinley, how—who could—"

McKinley leaned on his rake. His shoulders seemed to sag with the weight of his grief. His eyes remained fixed on the horizon. His face muscles worked. "I doan know, Mist' Davey I just doan know. Yest'day with the rain an' all I didn't look when I left—she could be gone then. I hurry along because I had do some shopping in Norwalk."

He spoke as though reciting a piece. Davey sensed that he had gone over things so often in his mind that every movement was memorized.

"I had to park a ways down the street from the market and

I was in there some little time—she could of been took then. Most times when I get home I take 'er out and look at 'er, maybe smell that fine leather a little. But last night, what with the rain and them bundles and all, I just put the car in the garade and run for the house. They's no lock on the garade; tell the truth they's only one door, so she could of been tooken durin' the night.

"Mist' Davey," he began, "do you reckon—"

But Davey wasn't there. He stumbled into the house and threw himself on Aunt Agatha.

"No, darling," she soothed, "you mustn't. *Please* don't make me cry again. I must go to an Altar Guild luncheon and I simply can't go all swelled up like a red-eyed hoptoad."

Rose was in the doorway. "That man just breaks my heart," she said. "He been lookin' forward to Sunday like a li'l child waitin' for Christmas or somethin'. McKinley ain't got too much sense, but he's such a *good* man. 'Tain't just a wallet itself, it's knowin' there's people walkin' the earth can be so lowdown *mean*."

"Now *you!*" Aunt Agatha exclaimed, almost sharply. She rose and went hastily into her study. "Run along, both of you," she called. "At least I can do *something*." Davey heard her blow her nose, lift the telephone receiver, and dial a number.

He got a book and went out on the terrace. He couldn't bear to face McKinley's grieving eyes. He couldn't bear to think of what, he felt sure, had happened to the wallet. It must have been a good book, for he was fairly well absorbed in it when Aunt Agatha came down to go to her luncheon.

"Do try to cheer up McKinley if you can, dear," she said. "I think we may be able to help some. I'll be home by four." Her car rolled down the drive, and Davey went back to his book.

Rose, still downcast, brought his lunch out to the terrace. "He got so little," she said, looking off across the fields. "He work so hard and with all them children he got so little for pleasure. I don't think in his whole life anythin' ever pleasured him like that present."

"Gee, Rose, you'll just ruin my Walls!" Davey tried to laugh.

"I know," she said. "Reckon Miss Agtha's right about 'em. My stummick's been like a nest o' yellowjackets all day. Guess I ought to stop thinkin' about it, but somehow it just make me so downright mad."

Davey finished his lunch and went back to his book. About midafternoon McKinley started cultivating the rosebeds near the terrace and Davey went out to talk with him. To the hurt look in McKinley's eyes there now seemed to be added a certain puzzlement.

"Mist' Davey," he asked, "you reckon I was too *proud* of that wallet? Sometimes in church I hear the parson talk 'bout how pride and vainglory is sins. Maybe I was too proud and vainglorious. Maybe I deserven to be laid low."

"That's silly," Davey said. "Why, look, didn't Father send you that wallet all the way from London? He picked out a good handsome one and had your initials put on it. And he did it because he liked you and thought you deserved it. Well, I think that ought to make anyone as proud as the dickens. There aren't many people he'd do that for. You've got a right to be as proud as you want to."

"Reckon you're right," McKinley agreed. "I shore was proud, but I'm laid low now."

Aunt Agatha returned and Davey joined her on the terrace. "How was the luncheon?" he asked.

"Oh, about as usual. That awful Mrs. Parling had some idiotic ideas and I had to put her in her place quite sharply. I'm afraid I shocked the Reverend."

"That wouldn't be hard," Davey commented.

She was about to reprove him when a station taxi sped up the drive. A young man dismounted and approached.

"Miss Martin?" he asked. "From Carradine and Price." He handed Aunt Agatha a small package.

"Oh, that's splendid!" She smiled. "Won't you sit down?"

"Thank you," the young man answered, glancing at his wristwatch, "but I can just make the four-two back to town. I'm sure you will find everything quite satisfactory." He hurried off, and Aunt Agatha broke the seals and opened the package.

Inside a stout cardboard box were several layers of white tissue paper. When these were removed there lay exposed a beautiful pigskin wallet. It was almost identical with the London one—if anything somewhat handsomer. It had the same rich smell, the same gold-leaf monogram "McK.W." Stamped in one corner, in tiny letters, were the words "Made in England." Davey stared at it in amazement.

"It's a wonderful thing," Aunt Agatha said happily, "to be the sister of the famous John Martin and sister-in-law to the beloved Garda Garrison, bless them. Carradine and Price is normally closed on Saturday, but those magic names tore their manager from the golf links and accomplished all this. I do hope the poor man finished his game."

She slipped a new dollar bill into one of the compartments and handed the wallet to Davey. "You must give it to him, dear," she said. "I will *not* shed tears again today."

Davey raced out to the rose garden. "Look what Aunt Agatha got you, McKinley," he cried, proffering the wallet. "It's almost exactly the same, and there's a dollar in it for the collection plate."

McKinley wiped his hands on his shirt and took it. His eyes were unbelieving. He stroked the smooth leather and smelled its rich aroma. His forefinger, trembling slightly, traced the stamped monogram. "McK.W.," he breathed, and then, "Mist' Davey, I *got* to speak to Miss Agtha."

"Well, McKinley?" Miss Agatha smiled from the terrace. "Of course it's not exactly the same, but I do hope it will serve."

McKinley turned the package over and over in his hands. His eyes again sought the horizon and his face muscles worked. "Maybe 'tain't *exactly* the same—but, Miss Agtha, I do thank you." He paused, searching for words. "All this day I been in the Valley of Despond and you've raise me out of it, an' I do thank you." He searched for more words, then abruptly departed. There was some spring in his steps now and the sag had left his shoulders.

"*Now!* He's done it again!" Aunt Agatha laughed shakily. "Davey, go take a bath." She hastened up to her room.

Dinner was a happier affair, but Davey's mind still buzzed with doubts and fears and indecisions. Aunt Agatha, sensing his upset, proposed the movies. "There's a picture I'd very much like to see," she said.

Which was a triple white lie. For she hadn't the slightest idea of what picture was being shown, there was almost never a picture she wanted to see, and she particularly disliked the movies on Saturday nights. However, Davey accepted gladly.

They arrived a few minutes before the nine o'clock show and managed to find seats about halfway down. Davey sat on the aisle.

As the feature and the newsreel ended the early comers began leaving. Davey was suddenly aware of Sonny Boy coming up the aisle, accompanied by four or five young village louts. As usual they were guffawing, pushing each other around, and lighting cigarettes. Sonny Boy wore a lilac-colored sport shirt, open at the neck, and a pair of pale green rayon slacks. Spying Davey, he saluted condescendingly and said, "Hiya, kid."

The group was held up momentarily. Sonny Boy's hip was less than a foot from Davey's face. Davey's breath suddenly stopped, and a cold sinking feeling gripped him. For, clearly as though he held it in his hand, he smelled McKinley's wallet. The fine pungent aroma of the pigskin was unmistakable. As they moved on he turned his head and was almost sure he could see the revealing outline in Sonny Boy's hip pocket.

For one moment Davey was gripped by a wild impulse to leap up and grapple with him, to snatch the wallet or shout "Stop Thief!" Pat Driscoll, the village cop, was in the lobby; he would help. Then he sank back helplessly. To start a brawl in the movies while accompanying Aunt Agatha was unthinkable. Besides, there was the faint possibility that his nose had played him false. Sonny Boy *might* have a similar wallet, honestly acquired, that smelled the same. That would be a fine mess!

And McKinley *did* have his new wallet. Davey felt sure he would prefer it to one that had been sullied by the hands of Sonny Boy.

The picture was far better than Aunt Agatha could have anticipated, and they both enjoyed it very much.

7. The Professor

For some time now Aunt Agatha had been insisting that they really must go in to New York for a few days of shopping. Davey had outgrown most of last summer's clothes, and she, of course, was going around in positive rags, although to Davey she always seemed beautifully dressed. She didn't say so, but she also felt that a short change would do them both good and help erase the memory of the recent unpleasant happenings, happenings so foreign to the usual quiet peace of Lavender Hill.

So they went in to town on Monday and had a wonderful four days. They stayed at the hotel where Mother and Father lived when they were in New York. The manager, of course, knew Aunt Agatha and made a great to-do over them, saw that they had beautiful rooms and everything they wanted.

When they weren't shopping they went to movies or the theater. They saw the opening of a new English film starring Mother, and everyone raved over her beauty and her acting. Davey thought that with all that make-up on she didn't look nearly so beautiful as at home, and her acting seemed, to him, just plain silly. It made him feel quite embarrassed. Aunt Agatha loved it though and cried at all the sentimental parts, as did most of the rest of the audience.

Skinny Ramsey and his mother came down and had lunch with them. They were going to Cape Cod for August and insisted that Davey come for a visit. He half promised, but he didn't think he'd really go; he liked it better at home.

Davey thoroughly enjoyed the New York food too. While Rose was a wonderful cook, the menu at Lavender Hill was usually fairly simple and necessarily limited. And, of course, the food at Elder Brewster Academy!

So Davey, usually egged on by the headwaiter, indulged in all sorts of rich and unfamiliar dishes. Strangely enough,

Aunt Agatha cast aside all thought of the Walls, never re-proved Davey, and went on a mild eating spree of her own.

On Tuesday evening they had just settled for dinner when Davey saw Aunt Agatha recognize someone. He turned and found a man approaching their table. He was of early middle age, lean, and of medium height. His slightly graying hair and mustache were closely cropped, his skin was well weather-browned and somewhat lined.

"Well, Miss Martin of all people," he greeted them. "Isn't this the usual thing—neighbors just over the hill and we have to come to New York to meet again." He smiled at Davey and Davey decided he liked him.

"Darling," Aunt Agatha said, "this is our neighbor Professor Benton, and, Professor, this is my nephew Davey."

"Hello," the Professor said. "Your aunt has told me about you. I hope she hasn't told you much about me—if anything."

"Are you all alone?" Aunt Agatha asked. "We would be delighted to have you join us."

"I can think of nothing more pleasant," he said, seating himself. "And now, what are you doing in the city?"

"Oh, shopping and this and that," Aunt Agatha replied. "And you?"

"The same thing," he said. "I feel it my duty to come in to the city once in a while, chiefly for the pleasure of going home."

A captain and a couple of waiters were hovering around, so they all ordered ridiculously indigestible dishes. The

Professor smiled at Aunt Agatha. "Of course," he said, "I know that such an ill-considered meal should have a frightful effect on the walls of the stomach, especially when one is tired, and I am quite worn out—from doing nothing. There is nothing so exhausting as doing nothing."

Aunt Agatha colored slightly and laughed. "We're taking a short vacation from the Walls, Professor Benton. So far without the slightest ill effect."

It was a delightful dinner. The Professor talked quite a bit, but it was all pleasant and amusing. He asked Davey a lot of questions about school—*not* the sort of questions that the Reverend Beasley always asked.

"Is McIlhenny still there?" he inquired. "And has he still got that old Buick? And what about Parks, and Carver?"

"Yes, sir, they're all there," Davey answered. "And Professor McIlhenny still has the old Buick—I guess it's the same one. It leaks oil and smokes and smells terribly, but it gets around."

"That's the one!" The Professor laughed, "Must be a museum piece by now. But old Mac isn't. Good egg, Mac, one of the best Greek scholars in the country. Taking Greek yet? Well, don't. And how about the food—awful as ever?"

"The food at Elder Brewster Academy is excellent for a growing boy," Aunt Agatha protested. "I went into it thoroughly. They have a highly skilled dietitian, and the meals, although simple, are very wholesome and nourishing."

"So are bread and water," Professor Benton said, laughing. "But I wasn't any growing boy when I taught there. Lost eighteen pounds and have never gained it back, although I try hard, I try hard." He speared a large piece of lobster from Davey's plate and replaced it with a small bit of his fish. "There, my boy, taste that morsel from heaven and pity the soul of old Elder Brewster, reared on cold clam cakes and boiled potatoes. His wholesome and nourishing spirit still goes marching on. Good old Brewster! And a murrain on the highly skilled dietitian!"

Aunt Agatha asked if he had seen the new English picture.

"Indeed yes," he answered. "Twice. One of the chief reasons I came to town. I haven't missed a Garda Garrison picture or play since there were any. Wasn't much of a plot, but she was magnificent. I sniffled just as loudly as the rest of the idiotic audience." He turned to Davey.

"I hope you don't mind if I confess to being your mother's most ardent admirer? I like your father's work too—about the best there is at present. I've written several articles on it, which he was kind enough to thank me for. Few ever bother to. And despite all this devotion I have never actually met either of them. I am looking forward to their next return to Lavender Hill. I shall come over with my smeary little autograph album, like any bobby-soxer and whine, 'Ple-e-e-z-e, Miss Garrison.'"

"At least you know their son," said Aunt Agatha, laughing, "and their sister/sister-in-law."

"Not as well as I hope to," Professor Benton said. "But—" He was stopped, somewhat aghast, by the arrival of the

mountainous dessert Davey had ordered. The Professor looked
hard at Aunt Agatha. *"Joshua fit the battle of Jericho,"* he
hummed, quite loudly, *"and the Walls come—tumblin' down."*

Davey and Aunt Agatha were going to the theater, so the
Professor parted from them in the lobby. "For myself," he
said, "I shall see the Garda Garrison picture again—this will
be the third time. I hope you will mention that when you
next write. By the way, Davey, what are you doing tomorrow
morning?"

Aunt Agatha had several fittings for the morning, but Davey
had no special plans. "Wonder if you'd care to come up to the
Metropolitan with me. Promised to see Carrington. They've
just acquired some wonderful guns. Know anything about
guns?"

"Well," Davey said, "I've got a twenty-two rifle, but I don't
get much chance to shoot it."

Professor Benton smiled. "These are hardly the same thing,"
he said. "Suppose you meet me here at ten?"

As usual, their taxi was held up by traffic in a side street.
While they inhaled gasoline fumes Aunt Agatha said, "I really
think Professor Benton is most charming, don't you?"

"He's swell," Davey replied. "I like him lots. What did he
mean about guns?"

"I understand he has made a hobby of collecting antique
firearms. He is supposed to have a priceless collection. People

say he spends most of his time and practically all his money on it."

Davey laughed. "Gee, no wonder he didn't think much of my twenty-two!"

Next morning Davey met the Professor and they took a taxi up to the Metropolitan Museum. On the way Professor Benton said, "Your aunt may have mentioned that I collect old fire-arms, in a very modest way, of course, but I do have a few rather choice ones.

"Many of my friends consider it a barbaric, bloodthirsty, and childish hobby. To them, beauty of line, exquisite work-manship, and romance mean nothing. For example, I have a handsome pistol used by one of John Paul Jones' lieutenants in the engagement of the *Bon Homme Richard* and the *Serapis*. To balance that in your hand and think of the history it has seen and helped to make gives you a tremendous thrill, at least it does me. I think it would anyone. But when I dis-played it to a stockbroker friend one day recently his only comment was, 'Say, are you sure this thing isn't loaded?'

"Carrington's a good egg, you'll like him," the Professor went on. "Knows his stuff too, none better. Of course the Metropolitan's collection is huge—makes mine look like pea-nuts. But I have a few that old Carrington would give his eyeteeth for. Thought you might like to look around while we gossip. It might give you a slight idea of the sort of work-manship those old boys turned out."

Mr. Carrington proved as pleasant and easygoing as the Professor, not at all what Davey had expected a curator to be like. They were introduced, and the Professor added, "Young Davey knows little about firearms yet, but he has an honor far greater than all your degrees and mine put together. It just happens that he is the son of Garda Garrison."

"Good Heavens," Mr. Carrington cried, "it can't be! Yes it can. There *is* a certain resemblance. Young man, may I confess that I am one of your mother's most ardent admirers?"

"You and a few million others." Professor Benton laughed. "I used that line last night. Have you seen the new picture?"

"Of course, twice," the Curator said. "It's magnificent."

"I'm one up on you," Professor Benton said. "I've seen it three times. Bill, I thought Davey might look around while we gab. Get an inkling of the wonders of ancient gunsmithing."

"Fine," Mr. Carrington said, "Couldn't be a better place to start him right." He called to a young man who was working at a desk. "Foster, suppose you show young Mr. Martin around. Start at the beginning and explain simply. You know, just the rudiments, of course."

Mr. Foster was slightly bald, wore glasses, and had a most serious manner. He looked at Davey as though he were some strange, rare specimen as he led him out to the galleries. "I'm sorry, Mr. Martin," he said hesitantly, "but I couldn't help overhearing Professor Benton's remarks. Is your mother *really* Garda Garrison?"

"Yes, she really is." Davey chuckled.

Mr. Foster's pale eyes, behind the thick glasses, took on a rapturous look. *"Gosh!"* he murmured. Then he showed Davey the collection most efficiently.

He started with the hand cannon and proceeded through matchlocks, wheel locks, snaphances, and flintlocks. He showed and explained harquebuses, musketoons, muskets, blunderbusses, sporting guns, and rifles. He took priceless pistols from their display cases and showed Davey how they worked. There were hundreds of pistols; Turkish, French, German, Spanish, and Dutch, all elaborately inlaid with gold and bone and ivory. There were simpler but beautifully made English pistols of every sort. There were large naval pistols with long belt hooks and heavy brass butts. There were tiny silver-inlaid pocket pistols, pistols with bayonets which sprang out when you touched the trigger guard. There were traveling pistols and dueling pistols in elaborately fitted cases.

Davey was almost dizzy with this wealth of beautiful design and workmanship. Mr. Foster showed him a sundial, made once for a King of France. There was a tiny bronze cannon mounted on it, exquisitely engraved. A small burning glass was adjusted so that exactly at noon it would focus the sun's rays on the touch hole and fire a salute.

"Professor Benton has one," Mr. Foster said. "Not quite as fine an example as this, of course, but a very good one. He will probably demonstrate it for you sometime."

He showed Davey the armory where they cleaned and repaired the various items of the collection. There was a long workbench with lathes, drills, screw-machines, vises, anvils, and lots of old-fashioned, unfamiliar tools. Seated at the bench was a little old gnome-like man, busily filing a pistol hammer.

"This is Adolph," Mr. Foster said. "He really belongs back in the middle ages. He is one of the few surviving true craftsmen. And one of the few who really loves his work."

Adolph removed his glasses and smiled pleasantly at Davey and Mr. Foster. "Yah, I like it here," he sighed. "One time I work in automobile factory; ossembly lines, stamp presses, big mout' foremen, union bosses, noise, noise, hurry, hurry, all the time. Phooie! Now I work good. Quiet, nice, careful. Old-fashioned way." He replaced his glasses and resumed his filing.

When they arrived back at the office the Curator and the Professor were in the midst of a hot argument. "I tell you it can't possibly be a Manton," the Professor shouted. "Where's the signature?"

"I've tried to get it through your thick skull about the signature," the Curator shouted back. "For two years Manton was in trouble with his Guild and—oh, here's our young friend. Well, Davey, how did you enjoy our little collection?"

"It's wonderful," Davey answered. "I didn't know there were that many guns in the world."

Mr. Carrington drew a small pistol from a drawer. "If you've really been bitten by the bug," he said, "here's

something to start your collection on." He slid the pistol across the desk to Davey.

"Bill, that's a very handsome gun," the Professor protested.

"It is," Mr. Carrington answered, "an extremely handsome gun. But it's not a Twigg. I bought it for a Twigg and it ought to be a Twigg, but it isn't. I got stuck, or rather the Museum got stuck. It's no use to us if it's not authentic, no matter how handsome."

Mr. Foster wrapped it up neatly, Davey thanked him and the Curator politely, and they took their leave. All the way down to the hotel Davey, clutching his precious package, felt almost in a daze. It seemed as though he had been back in medieval times all morning. The rushing buses and taxis and rasping horns seemed completely unreal.

"By George," Professor Benton chuckled, "that's the first time I ever saw old Bill give away anything in his life. It's wonderful, my boy, to be Garda Garrison's son. Of course there's something in being a nice, decent, well-mannered young guy too."

8. Benton's Elements

The only thing that had bothered Davey in the city was the smells. There were so many hundreds of them that he felt confused all the time. Not that all of them were bad. There were many beautiful perfume and powder odors when one walked along the avenues, and delightful smells from many of the shops, especially the candy and cake stores. But there were many that were not so pleasant. Basement openings, subway ventilators, manholes and lunchroom fans poured forth stenches that were, to Davey, almost overpowering. And of course there was the ever-present choking medley of motor exhausts, oil burners, and coal smoke.

Once or twice when they passed luggage shops a pungent whiff of leather would bring an unhappy thought of the lost field glass and the missing wallet, but the twinge was only momentary. On the whole, the busy, happy four days had quite wiped out the unpleasant memories, just as Aunt Agatha had hoped they would. In all probability he would not see Sonny Boy again all summer. He would forget the whole thing.

Now, as they rolled up the drive at Lavender Hill, it was good to be back among the pleasant, simple country smells; smells that he could recognize and trace. His nose located a woodchuck burrow near the stone gatepost—that must be a new one. There had been some showers, and the new grass springing up in the cut-over hayfields smelled fresh and sweet. As they approached the house he could smell McKinley's old Ford, and there was a delightful whiff of frying chicken on the air.

McKinley was waiting in the drive to greet them and carry in the bags. He was beaming happily, just as of old. "My goodness, Miss Agtha," he chuckled as he lifted the bags from the car, "my wallet certainly were a sensation. Don't think there's been as much excitement in that old church sence we got the new organ. *Every*body want to see a wallet come all the way from London, England. Ain't one of 'em got one with they own letters on it, 'cept the pastor, and them only little ol' brass ones. I do thank you Miss Agtha."

The house glittered with cleanliness and, as always, was sweet with the odor of lavender. There was a stack of mail on the hall table which Davey sniffed in passing. "There's a letter from Mother," he announced. "She's got a new perfume. And I think there's one from Goofer Wallace. He always stinks of birds' eggs and snake skins and stuff."

He hugged Aunt Agatha. "I had a wonderful time," he said, "but it's nice to be home too. It smells so good."

Aunt Agatha sniffed the air and laughed. "Lavender and furniture polish *and* fried chicken may seem an odd combination, but they do smell like home."

Rose too was in high spirits. Her niece and nephew had stayed with her during the family's absence. Aunt Agatha complimented her on the shining cleanliness of the house.

"I've had a vacation too," she said. "I promised to teach them young ones to cook and clean, and believe me I *taught* 'em. I haven't raised my hand these four days."

Next morning Davey presented McKinley with two neckties he had brought from New York. "There now, McKinley, now you can *really* knock 'em dead."

"I sho will," McKinley chuckled, regarding them admiringly. "I sho will. A wallet from London, England. Long elegant seegars from Havana, Cuba. A blue coat from

Hollywood, California, and now neckties from New York City. I certainly am geography outfitted."

After lunch Davey decided to go over and call on Professor Benton. He had liked him tremendously, he was ever so grateful for the pistol from the Metropolitan, and he was eager to see the Professor's collection. He wandered over the hill and down through the fields to the old Barker place. As he approached the air was heavy with the scent of roses.

The Professor had indeed done wonders with the old place. As Davey vaguely remembered it, it had been a fairly small house, square and flat roofed and painted a bilious yellow-brown. It had always been run-down, streaked and damp-looking, overgrown with trees and creepers.

Now the trees and brush had been cleared away, except for a few fine maples and elms. The sun shone on velvet green lawns, neatly clipped shrubs, and a crisp graveled driveway. The house itself glistened in new white paint, sharp black shutters, ruffled white curtains. There seemed to be a new wing on one side, almost as large as the original house. The wing had a stone-paved terrace before it and two huge, studio-like windows. Back of the house were two flower gardens surrounded by low stone walls.

In one of these, apparently devoted to roses, a tall, gaunt man was working. He straightened up at Davey's hail and regarded him solemnly. His long face reminded Davey of an old and rather unhappy horse.

"Professor Ben-tin?" he said in a slow Maine drawl. "Sure.

Find him right there in his study." He flicked his thumb in the direction of the new wing. "Gaowin' to rain?"

Davey sniffed the air. "I don't think so," he answered. "I don't smell any."

"Don't think so neither," the man said sadly and went back to his digging. "Need it," he added.

Davey knocked on the screen door and at a shouted "Come in" opened it and entered. The Professor was seated at a large combination desk and workbench beside one of the tall windows. At Davey's entrance he rose and greeted him cordially.

"Well, well," he cried, "back from the city all safe and sound—including the Walls, I hope. Sit down, sit down.

"I came out yesterday," he went on, after they were comfortably settled. "Began to get worried about what Meeker might do, or not do, to the roses. Did you see him in the garden as you came by?"

"Yes, sir," Davey answered. "He was cultivating the roses. He told me where to find you."

"Cultivating?" The Professor laughed. "That's fine. Just what I wanted. I told him to spray. You see, Meeker's fine and all that, but he does treasure his independence. If I tell him to spray he cultivates, and if I tell him to cultivate he sprays. Today they needed cultivating badly so I suggested he might spray. So he cultivates. It's a perfectly good system—once you get used to it."

All the time that the Professor was talking Davey was looking with interest at the room, which was unlike any he had ever seen. It was quite high ceilinged, with two huge windows at the north end. Before one of these stood a workbench with anvils, vises, and old tools, much like those in the armory at the Metropolitan. Before the other was the Professor's desk and workbench. On it were a few tools, a great many books, a magnifying glass, a vase of roses, a telephone, and a typewriter. The latter two objects, the only modern things in the room, seemed strangely out of place.

A great old-fashioned fireplace took up most of one wall. In it, beside the cranes and pothooks, were several crucibles filled with lead, a small forge, and more tools. Hung from the mantel were dozens of bullet molds of various shapes and sizes. The remaining wall space was occupied by cabinets of shallow drawers, topped by flat glass showcases. These contained the Professor's collection of pistols, revolvers, shot flasks, and powder horns. Above the cabinets were racks where hung the long arms: muskets, rifles, carbines, blunderbusses, and sporting guns. Here and there, between the racks, were brackets holding fascinating ship models. There was also a set of bookshelves containing his library of books dealing with arms and armor.

An enormous old gray-striped tomcat came from somewhere and approached Davey. It circled his ankles, sniffing, while the Professor watched closely. Finally the cat rubbed against Davey's leg, hopped up on the broad arm of his chair, and settled down, purring contentedly. The Professor relaxed.

"Good," he said. "He approves of you. His name is Andrew Jackson and, like his famous namesake, he has a somewhat uncertain temper and violent likes and dislikes. If he likes you he is your friend for life. If he does not—watch your step. When certain of my friends call, Andrew has to be locked in the closet. Strangely enough they affect me the same way.

"And now," he went on, "I would be delighted to show off my collection."

Compared to the Metropolitan's, it was, perhaps, a small collection, but to Davey it seemed overwhelming. The Professor explained all its items in detail, so the afternoon was almost gone before they had finished.

A short, round, pleasant-faced woman poked her head in at the door and, gazing at the ceiling, recited, "We've got chocolate cake, cookies, milk, ginger ale, tea or coffee, hot or iced."

"Iced tea, thanks," the Professor said. "What's yours, Davey?"

Davey decided on cake and a glass of milk. The lady departed.

"Mrs. Meeker," the Professor explained. "For many years she ran a lunchroom somewhere in Maine, which accounts for her formal delivery. A good soul though, as cheerful as Meeker is lugubrious. And a wonderful cleaner, which endears her to me. Her cooking is not exactly inspired and smacks somewhat of the hash house days, but I do pretty well."

While they sipped their refreshments the Professor put his feet up on his desk and went on talking.

"Davey," he said suddenly, "from your complete lack of animosity I can only judge that you have not yet learned the worst about me. By most boys—and girls—I am probably the most hated man in America, yet you seem to regard me quite kindly. Don't you know who I am?"

"Why, no," Davey answered, "I just know you taught Latin at Brewster and that you live here—that's all."

"In your Latin studies at Brewster haven't you been afflicted, lacerated, bored, and harried by a horrid book entitled *Benton's Elements of Latin Grammar*?"

"Oh," Davey said in a small voice, "oh—yes."

"I see you grasp the connection. Now you know all. *I* am that Benton. I wrote the thing. Let me explain.

"When I first taught at Brewster I was young, ambitious, filled with energy and an adoration of Latin. There were few good Latin grammars, so I decided to write the perfect one. I spent my nights, my weekends, and my vacations at it. It was a good book, an excellent textbook—it still is. And it was successful, fantastically successful—and still is. It has been used in thousands of schools, in hundreds of thousands of copies—and still is.

"It makes me smile, nowadays, when some work of fiction is hailed as a 'best seller.' Why, the State of Missouri alone consumes, over the years, more copies of the *Elements* than any of these flashes in the pan. And there are forty-eight states in these United States, not to mention Alaska, Hawaii, and the Philippines.

"Royalties flowed in in unbelievable amounts—and still do. I was in danger of becoming wealthy, and to make matters worse a great-uncle, whom I scarcely knew, died and left me his considerable fortune, and a safety-pin factory. The demand for safety-pins is, of course, as enduring as the demand for *Benton's Elements,* so I seem fated to have two never-failing sources of income.

"I could see, however, that my teaching days were numbered, and I really loved teaching. But it became a daily agony to look on the hurt, reproachful faces of my students when they dragged out their *Benton's* and resentfully went to work. It was during that period that I lost those eighteen pounds.

"I tried to persuade the Board of Brewster Academy to substitute some other Latin grammar, but they were adamant. None could compare to mine. So I resigned. I tried in vain to find some school which did not use it, but there wasn't any. I even considered changing my name and growing a beard, but I couldn't raise an impressive-looking one, and besides it was awfully scratchy.

"I gave up teaching. I turned over my financial affairs to my Cousin Harold, who is an investment banker and actually likes that sort of thing. I have no idea of what I am worth financially, which is grand, for it is harrying to feel poor and most upsetting to feel rich. He sends me an allowance for my needs and always comes across when I demand an extra sum for some cherished piece for my collection, so I'm sure I am still solvent.

"For some years I traveled, pretty much all over the world. During those years I became interested in collecting old fire-arms, and also in growing roses. I needed a house for my collection and a garden for roses—so here I am. And there is my sad tale. I do hope this confession will not blight a friend-ship so auspiciously begun."

Davey finished his cake. He stroked Andrew Jackson's head, and Andrew flexed his claws, digging them sleepily into the chair arm. "I don't think it will," Davey said, laughing. "It *is* a pretty tough book, but I won't have to see it again till fall."

The Professor laughed too, got up, and extracted a book from the shelves. "Here is a book that is *not* tough," he said, "if you're really interested in guns. It will give you a very good understanding of the whole general subject. Take it along and read it."

Davey thanked him, gave Andrew Jackson a last stroke, and departed. As he passed the rose garden Mr. Meeker straightened up and regarded him sorrowfully. "Gaowin' to rain?" he asked.

"I don't think so," Davey answered. "I don't smell any."

"Don't think so neither." Mr. Meeker sighed. "Need it though." He went back to his digging, and Davey ran on home over the hill.

9. The Happy Apprentice

Aunt Agatha was curious to hear about the Professor's house and garden, so during and after dinner Davey told her all that he could remember about them. It was not a very satisfactory account, however, for he had not seen any of the house except the study and hadn't paid much attention to the gardens.

"I do wish you had had a glimpse of the rest of the house," Aunt Agatha said. "I understand he has superb antiques and

85

some priceless china and glass. And next time you go over, do look at the roses more carefully."

She was not especially interested in the weapon collection, but she was interested in the Professor's life story as recounted by Davey. "I thought he seemed like a well-traveled person," she said. "But I do think he somewhat exaggerated the effects of his Latin grammar on his students."

"Oh, no, he didn't. You've never used *Benton's Elements of Latin Grammar*. He was awfully funny about it though, and about the Meekers too."

"I'm glad she is a good cleaner," Aunt Agatha mused. "We must have him over for dinner soon. I am sure he would appreciate Rose's cooking."

Davey went over to see the Professor the next day and the next, in fact almost every day during the rest of the summer. The path through the hayfields soon became well worn.

Professor Benton had acquired several new guns during the New York visit and was now busy cleaning and putting them in shape. He showed Davey how to take them apart, how to remove rust gently with a razor blade, how to clean with paraffin oil, emery, crocus powder, and the finest steel wool. He taught him how to polish with rouge, brass polish, furniture polish, and, most of all, elbow grease.

"Many people use an electric buffing wheel," the Professor said, "which does a perfectly good job. Personally, I prefer to rub by hand. It is quiet, restful, and excellent mental discipline."

"Like studying Latin." Davey laughed. "That's what they always tell us at school."

Davey had one workbench, the Professor the other. All morning, or all afternoon, perched on a high stool, Davey would happily rub and scrape, oil and polish, while the Professor talked.

He told Davey endless tales of the old gunsmiths and their methods. He produced ancient engravings which showed their crude, hand-driven machines for turning, boring, and screw-making. He explained how they did their inlaying, etching, engraving, damascening, tempering, browning, and bluing. He told of the laborious duties of the apprentices of those days, he showed old contracts stipulating their hours of work and rest, of what subsistence the master must provide.

"It *was* pretty rugged," the Professor admitted. "A twelve-hour day and two shillings a year would not appeal to the young squirts of today, but, by George, it produced artists and craftsmen who have never been equaled."

Whenever the Professor was working on some gun which had a special historical connection he would drift into an account of that occasion. Working on the John Paul Jones pistol he recounted for a whole delightful afternoon the engagement of the *Bon Homme Richard* and the *Serapis*.

He told it well. Davey could hear the heavy thud of the

guns in the *Richard's* rotting old gundecks, the tearing crash of the *Serapis's* broadsides, the screaming boarding parties, the rattle of small arms from the fighting tops. He could smell the thick powder smoke, the burning timbers, the flaming rigging. He could picture himself a sweating powder monkey, racing endlessly up and down blood-slimy companionways, his bare feet torn by splinters, burned by smoldering ropes, lugging his precious leather buckets of powder; or carrying buckets of water to fight the fires, buckets of sand to spread on the red-wet floor of the lazaret, where the surgeons and their mates hacked and sawed and bandaged.

Or perhaps it was a long Kentucky rifle the Professor was working on, and Davey would be an enthralled spectator at turkey shoots along the Yadkin or see the trappers from Tennessee and Kentucky behind their cotton-bale breastworks at the battle of New Orleans, as side by side with Lafitte's pirates they calmly and efficiently picked off the British officers with incredible marksmanship.

Or perhaps a clumsy naval pistol would wake a tale of Morgan or Kidd or Blackbeard. It was a seaman's pistol like this, perhaps this very one, which had finally felled Blackbeard and allowed Lieutenant Maynard to hack off his head and nail it to the bowsprit of his sloop.

The sack of Panama, Lexington, Concord, and Bunker Hill, the slaughter of the Alamo, Yorktown, and Gettysburg, all came alive and real to Davey, through the magic of these old guns and the Professor's pleasant voice.

"You know an awful lot about history," Davey said one day. "Why didn't you teach that after you gave up Latin?"

"I should have liked to." Professor Benton smiled. "It would be great fun if one could stick to only the interesting parts. Unfortunately, much of it is parliamentary debates, resolutions, acts, treaties, conventions, compromises, broken promises, and similar skulduggery. There's no fun in that."

They did a good deal of shooting too. The Professor insisted that every gun in his collection should be not only in perfect condition but really usable. So each new acquisition was thoroughly tested.

Out in the field beyond the rose garden he had had a shooting butt built, a high sodded rampart much like a bunker on a golf links. Before this was a stout post that supported a heavy steel shield. Beyond the shield was another post fitted with clamps to hold the gun being tested. Whenever a new gun arrived the Professor would load it with the heaviest possible charge, cramming it to the muzzle with black powder, wads, and ball. It was clamped to the post and then, while they crouched behind the shield, the Professor would slip a wire through a slit in the shield, hook it to the trigger, and pull.

There would be a tremendous explosion, then both would race around to see the results. With his magnifying glass the Professor would carefully examine the barrel for any flaws, cracks, or swelling. Three tests like this proved any gun safe for shooting with a normal load. Once in a great while a gun under test would explode, the barrel curling back in jagged strips like a peeled banana. It would be dismantled and the usable parts saved for repairs or replacements.

Sometimes they shot for pleasure. The Professor would take a pair of perfectly matched dueling pistols from their case. They would mold bullets, cut linen patches and grease them with tallow. They would load with the finest powder and shoot at targets all afternoon. The Professor, who was a crack shot, taught Davey the principles of stance, sighting, and trigger pull, and he soon became quite proficient.

Usually the Professor was Aaron Burr and Davey was Alexander Hamilton. At the end of the afternoon when they examined their targets and counted their scores the Professor would remark, "Well, Alex, you're improving, but still far deader than I am. I have put six bullets through your heart, two through your left lung, one in your gullet, and one between the eyes. Whereas you have punctured my heart only four times, my stomach once, my right hip twice, and wasted three shots entirely."

"All right, Aaron," Davey would retort, "I'll get you next time." Then they would clean and oil the pistols, and Mrs. Meeker would bring them cookies and milk.

During these long mornings and afternoons Davey told the Professor about his remarkable sense of smell. The Professor was greatly interested and kept devising new tests. Every day Davey had to tell him exactly what Mrs. Meeker was preparing for lunch or dinner, and although the kitchen was at

the extreme far end of the house he was always right. As the tests became more elaborate and more difficult the Professor's interest became even more intense. "By George," he exclaimed, "it's the most amazing gift I've ever encountered. It really should be put to some use."

"Skinny Ramsey wants me to go with the circus next summer. He says he's sure he can get us a job in a side show. He's my manager and he wants fifty per cent of anything we make. I think that's too much, and anyway I don't think Aunt Agatha would let me."

10. The Strap

Davey's gift was put to use sooner than they expected. Dropping into the study one afternoon, he found the Professor engaged in conversation with a large, heavy-set man. The man had reddish, almost curly hair, wore glasses, and had a firm

93

but kindly face. Davey took him to be a professor friend or some fellow collector and was quite surprised when Professor Benton introduced him as Lieutenant Corrigan of the State Police.

"He looks more impressive in uniform," the Professor said, laughing, "but he hates to wear one. Says it scares children.

"The Lieutenant and I are old pals," he went on. "I've helped teach the boys some of the rudiments of marksmanship—several of them have developed into excellent shots—all except Corrigan, of course. He's hopeless."

The Lieutenant leaned back in his deep chair and smiled tolerantly. "If you'd shoot with a civilized gun," he chuckled in a low gentle voice, "instead of those antique iron-age relics of yours, I could teach *you* a few rudiments."

His hand slid into the breast of his coat and immediately slid out, holding a service revolver. The movement was so smooth and rapid that Davey had scarcely seen it. The Lieutenant swung out the chamber and extracted the shells. He held the gun out to Davey.

"There, my boy," he said, "there's a *real* gun. Don't let the Professor here be fooling you with those old gas pipes of his. They're pretty and all that, but they don't shoot."

He stood the shells up on the arm of his chair and moved them about absently, as though they were chessmen. "The Professor," he went on, "has been telling me about your remarkable sense of smell. It seems hard to believe, but after you've been in this game for twenty years you can believe almost anything."

He pointed toward the Professor's desk, and Davey, for the first time, noticed a long narrow leather strap, laid out on a sheet of white paper.

"That bit of leather strap there now," the Lieutenant asked, "could you smell anything special about that?"

Davey didn't even move from his chair. "Why, I can smell dog on it from here," he said. "Is that what you mean? It's a dog's leash, isn't it?"

He saw the Professor and the Lieutenant exchange a quick glance. "I *told* you—" the Professor started, then subsided. Lieutenant Corrigan continued to move the shells around while he gazed out at the blue sky. "It could be a dog's leash," he admitted. "The loop and the snap are newly cut off. It could be a kid's bookstrap, or a strap from a pair of skis—it could be a lot of things." His voice was more gentle than ever as he turned again to Davey. "You wouldn't have an idea what kind of dog?"

Davey rose and approached the desk more closely, sniffing carefully. "I'm not sure I can tell *exactly*," he said. "Dogs smell pretty much alike. I'm sure it's not short-haired, they smell sort of sour. I *think* it's a German shepherd—yes, I'm pretty sure it is." The Lieutenant breathed a long sigh. He relaxed and leaned back in his chair, his hands clasped behind his head, his eyes on the sky beyond the big window. "Anything else?" he asked almost sleepily.

"Yes, there is," Davey said. He advanced still closer, sniffing more intently. "Oh, now I get it." He laughed. "Bakery. It should have been easy, I can smell a bakery half a mile away. But the dog smell was too strong. Oh, sure, I get it perfectly now. Bakery."

Andrew Jackson had settled in the Lieutenant's lap. The Lieutenant stroked his head for a moment, then rose and deposited him gently in Davey's chair. He picked up the shells, slipped them into the gun, and slid the gun under his coat.

"Use the phone, Professor?" he asked. He dialed a number, and they heard a crisp voice answer.

"Carey?" the Lieutenant said. "This is Corrigan. Look, remember the bird we were talking about this morning? On the Norwalk jewelry store job. I forget his name, but you know. Works in the bakery in New Canaan, has a German shepherd dog. Well, have a couple of the boys bring him in, and I mean bring him in—the hard way if they have to. We've got everything. And, wait a minute. While they're there, see if his dog's got a new leash and give the place a good look over. Okay, I'll be down shortly."

He hung up and settled in the deep chair again. Andrew Jackson came back to his lap. The Lieutenant absently scratched his ears and chin.

"Seeing as you've been such a big help," he said, "I guess I owe you the story. Yesterday evening there was a jewelry store held up in Norwalk. Little place run by an old German guy. Tied him up in the back room with that leather strap and then cleaned out the place. What was stolen didn't amount to much and most of it was insured.

"Well, we had our eye on two or three promising suspects, but nothing to go on except that leather strap. One of our suspects was a young bird over in New Canaan. He works in a bakery and lives in a room over the shop. Also, he has a German shepherd dog he's crazy about. Takes him out for exercise every night—on a leash. So your nose fixes everything. Dog leash, smells of German shepherd, smells of bakery. We're all set. It was a brilliant bit of smelling."

He wrapped the strap in the white paper and stuffed it in his pocket. He rested his hand on Davey's shoulder a moment. "Glad to have met you, son," he said. "You've got a great gift. So long, Professor, I'll be seeing you." He left, and a moment later they heard his car roll down the drive.

"It's funny," Davey said thoughtfully. "He's solved this holdup thing and got all his evidence and everything and you'd think he'd be excited over it. But he just seemed sort of tired and sad."

"I can see how it might be," the Professor said. "I think it would be like this. He has a case—a puzzle to solve. It's exciting and it must be done, it's his duty. He goes at it with everything he's got. Then, suddenly, it's solved. He has all the answers. Naturally there is a let-down. The rest of it is just sad and dreary.

"He has to face some trapped, terrified, probably stupid

young man. He has to confront him with the damning evidence. He has to watch him bluster and squirm and sweat and lie and finally wilt and probably confess. He may be some young ex-GI. He may have some desperate need for money. Corrigan has two boys of his own, one about your age, one sixteen. It might almost be one of them. It must be pretty harrowing, for a father. The older, hard-boiled, really criminal types don't bother him at all, but these young ones get him down. And so many these days are so young, so cocksure—and so stupid."

He sat a few moments in thought and then sprang up. "Let's think of something more pleasant," he said briskly. "Suppose I gather an elegant bouquet of roses for your charming aunt and suppose you ask her to come over for tea tomorrow. About five?"

Next morning the Professor had barely finished his breakfast when Lieutenant Corrigan arrived at the study. He looked tired and rumpled. He needed a shave badly.

"Wonder if Mrs. Meeker could spare a cup of coffee?" he asked, settling wearily in a chair.

Mrs. Meeker was already at the door with a large pot of coffee. "Okay, Loot," she greeted him cheerily. "Know how you boys on the night shift crave your java." Andrew Jackson settled on the arm of the chair. He sniffed idly at the cream pitcher, decided against it, and went to bathing.

"Well," said the Professor, "is the great jewel robbery all solved? What was it, the usual stupid story or just vicious?"

"Just the usual." The Lieutenant sighed, stirring his coffee. "A little stupider maybe. A young ex-GI. Crazy, hasty war marriage, two young kids.

"Wife took the kids and left him because he couldn't support them. He doesn't amount to much anyway. Had a job in this bakery—wasn't even good at that. They were going to fire him end of the month. Like I told you yesterday, he lived in a room over the shop and had a German shepherd dog he was crazy about—used to exercise him every evening, on a leash. That was the leash we had here. It smelled of dog and it smelled of bakery—it all fitted in." He poured another cup of coffee and slowly stirred it.

"So-o-o, the sap decided to do something big, make some quick money, be a smart guy, show the world. And he pulled this job. It wasn't very big and he wasn't very smart. The boys found all the stuff. He had it hidden in a couple of hollowed out loaves of bread, just like in a detective story. They even found the loop and the snap from the leash, the cuts fitted perfectly.

"Of course he talked big at first, but we faced him with all the facts and after a while he folded up. Made a full and free confession to the whole business. So it's all set."

The Lieutenant finished his coffee and rose wearily from the chair.

"I'll be getting along home for a bit of sleep," he sighed.

"Been up all night—and last night." He leaned down and scratched Andrew Jackson's jowls.

"What I really wanted to say, though, is about the young Martin lad. Things like this are liable to be upsetting to kids of his age. I never talk about cases to my young ones—isn't good for them. I wouldn't want him to know.

"Yesterday I just told you that that strap was used in this job, but I didn't say exactly how. It was ugly. The charge is murder."

11. Quiet Tea Party

Davey arrived shortly after the Lieutenant had left.

"Aunt Agatha's awfully sorry about this afternoon," he announced, "but she says she'd already invited the Reverend and couldn't you come over to us for tea? As a matter of fact," he added, "I think he invited himself, sort of. Anyway he's coming."

"Please convey my kindest regards to your aunt," the Professor said, "and tell her I will be delighted to come."

"Oh, grand," said Davey, "and there's plenty of sherry and stuff if you don't like tea. Father always has a mint julep if it's hot and, it's certainly going to be hot today. He says Rose makes a lollapalooza."

"Fine," said the Professor, "I will consider it seriously."

"Well, I've got to be going. I promised to go down town with Aunt Agatha. I'll see you this afternoon." He started for the door, then added, "I wonder how the Lieutenant came out?"

"Oh, all right," the Professor answered carelessly. "Just the usual stupid case. The man confessed. Didn't amount to much."

The tea party was gathered on the terrace. Aunt Agatha wore one of the new frocks acquired during the New York visit, and Davey was struck, almost for the first time, by the fact that she was really a lovely looking person. Not as spectacularly beautiful as Mother, of course, but still very lovely. The Professor and the Reverend Beasley seemed fully aware of this too.

It was really hot, even on the shaded terrace. The Professor's linen suit was already considerably rumpled.

Davey, well scrubbed, wore white shorts, an immaculate shirt, and, under protest, a necktie. McKinley had also scrubbed, and now in a white jacket, served with great dignity, although his eyes now and then rested longingly on the garden, where he would far rather have been. The tall frosty

glasses of iced tea, topped with fresh mint, looked so refresh-
ing that the Professor never even thought of Davey's offered
"lollapalooza."

"Professor Benton, your roses were simply superb," Aunt
Agatha was saying. "It was so thoughtful of you to send them
over, but they put my sad efforts to shame. How do you ever
manage it?"

"Some small effort on my part, and a great deal more on
Meeker's. But really you must come over and see for yourself."

"The rose has but a summer reign," the Reverend quoted.
"The daisy never dies." He took a tea cake. "We are dis-
appointed, Professor Benton, that you have not yet attended
our little services at Old Trinity."

"Sorry," the Professor apologized. "I should have, I have
really meant to, but every Sunday so far there seems to have
been some poor ailing rosebush crying for aid. Also, Meeker
has settled on Sunday morning as the only proper time to
clean the car, so I am without transport."

"Davey and I will be delighted to pick you up any Sunday,"
Aunt Agatha suggested.

"That," said the Professor, "places the matter in an entirely
new light. I will mend my ways, beginning this coming Sunday. About ten-thirty?"

"Splendid." Aunt Agatha smiled. "And now would you care
to see my few sorry roses?"

The Professor rose readily, and they strolled off toward the
rose garden.

"Well, David," the Reverend exclaimed heartily, "and what have you been up to this summer?"

"Oh, I've been helping the Professor with his guns mostly," Davey answered. "He's got a wonderful collection. I'm his apprentice. He lets me clean them and polish them, and we shoot them quite a lot."

The Reverend refilled his glass. "It seems too bad," he said, "that you cannot derive something more useful from this association. Latin, for example; Professor Benton is a well-known Latin scholar."

"But it's vacation," Davey protested. "Latin's no vacation. He's taught me a lot about guns, though, and lots about history; he knows an awful lot about history." He noisily sucked up the dregs of his iced tea and poured himself some more.

When the Professor and Aunt Agatha returned the Reverend was in the midst of a long discourse. Davey was sullenly blowing into his glass through the straw. It made a most unpleasant noise.

"I was just saying to David," the Reverend began, "that it seems a pity that his summer is not being devoted to Latin but to a study of lethal weapons. I would rather fear the impact of such brutalizing implements on the impressionable young mind." Davey made an even louder noise with his straw, and Aunt Agatha shushed him.

The Professor smiled. "I hardly think that studying guns will make Davey into a gunman," he said, "any more than studying the stars would turn an astronomer into a Peeping

Tom. I can't think of anything more beneficial to the impressionable young mind than an appreciation of fine workmanship and beauty. Old guns have about as much of those qualities as anything man-made. Of course in nature everything is beautiful, reaching a climax perhaps in roses—and Garda Garrison." He laughed pleasantly, but his eyes were on Aunt Agatha as he spoke.

At this moment McKinley's head and shoulders appeared around the corner of the house. He crooked his finger at Davey, then went through a short pantomime.

"Woodchuck!" Davey exclaimed. He rose hastily, jarring the tea table, and rushed into the house. He reappeared almost at once, loading his twenty-two, took the steps at one bound, and joined McKinley. They departed on tiptoe.

"The taking of human life—" the Reverend began.

"But, Doctor Beasley," Aunt Agatha interrupted him, "woodchucks are not exactly *human* life. We never bother them as a rule, but when one makes his home practically *in* the garden and devours row after row of vegetables, *something* has to be done."

The Professor leaned forward and touched her arm. "Look," he said quietly, "isn't that beautiful?"

McKinley and Davey were circling the end of a thick shrubbery border. McKinley on hands and knees led the way, smooth and tense as a big cat. Behind him Davey crept, his rifle held at a safe angle. McKinley paused and motioned Davey forward. They disappeared around the shrubbery.

"It's all the young hunters of the world," the Professor said, still quietly, "with their faithful guides or gunbearers. Leatherstocking, Daniel Boone, young Teddy Roosevelt."

There was a sudden sharp crack. The Professor listened intently, then smiled. "One good shot," he said, "or a clean miss. Woodchucks are tough."

A few minutes later Davey returned. He put his rifle away and rejoined the party. His white clothes had lost much of their immaculateness—there were quite a few grass stains. He resumed his iced tea and, smiling at the Professor, held up one finger. "One-shot Martin. Right through the heart. McKinley's going to skin him and take him home. He says his wife makes a wonderful pot-pie out of them. You have to take out some of the glands and things."

The Reverend looked rather squeamish, and Aunt Agatha said, *"Darling!"*

"The Meekers have the same weakness," said the Professor. "They have tried to tempt me many times, but I have always resisted with the greatest ease. Andrew Jackson, though, approves highly."

McKinley appeared with more cakes and fresh iced tea. The Reverend was just reaching for another cake when the far-off howl of the village fire siren rent the air. McKinley straightened up, and the Reverend was left reaching. In silence they all counted, "One—one—four."

McKinley tossed his tray on the table and sprinted. Davey, following, managed almost to upset the tea table. The

Professor snatched his glass, but the other glasses toppled, spilling their contents on the lovely cakes. The old Ford roared down the drive, scattering gravel and leaving a cloud of dust.

"One—one—four, that's in the village," Professor Benton said. He stepped out on the lawn where there was a clearer view to the south, and Miss Agatha joined him. Far away over the hill a narrow column of black smoke was rising. "By George," he exclaimed eagerly, "it looks like a good one! I'd like to—" He glanced at Aunt Agatha's parked car.

Her eyes sparkled and she took one step. "I would too," she said. Then she glanced toward the terrace. "But it wouldn't do." They rejoined the Reverend.

Rose appeared and mopped up the mess. "Them children," she chuckled. "Minute that old sireen hoot they lose what little sense they got."

"Miss Martin," the Reverend began, "doesn't this practice of David's of dashing to fires strike you as somewhat dangerous for—"

Again Aunt Agatha interrupted him, this time almost impatiently. "McKinley is an excellent driver," she said. "I do not know of a better. He often drives me when I feel it necessary to be impressive. He watches over Davey like a mother; far more intelligently than most. Besides, Chief Dolan and all his men know them well; they are both unofficial, unpaid, honorary members of Vigilant Company Number One. They will be well looked after."

After this the conversation threatened to languish, but

Professor Benton came gallantly to Miss Agatha's aid, chatting pleasantly and interestingly about China, India, roses, England, clipper ships, Japanese beetles, Irish poetry, the Meekers, sprays, fertilizers, politics, and the wonders of Rose's baking. Miss Agatha, appreciating his effort, smiled and encouraged him with occasional questions.

Davey finally returned and slumped wearily in his chair. His wet shoes squelched; from head to toe he was streaked with mud, oil, water, and slime. He helped himself to three cakes and fresh iced tea, sighing happily.

"It was a *really* good one," he recounted. "That hardware store on Elm Street. There was a lot of oil and turpentine and paint in the cellar, and it made a swell smoke—and did it burn! A lot of ammunition too that kept going off. Mr. Dolan let us help with a hose. That's how I got a little dirty." He smiled apologetically at Aunt Agatha. "McKinley's cleaning up; he'll be around in a minute." McKinley arrived, somewhat slicked up and with a fresh coat, but also squelchy as to shoes. However, he was not needed, it was time to go home. The Reverend bade them good-by. "We shall hope for your presence on Sunday, Professor," he said. "You, Miss Martin, we are always sure of—and David, of course." He slapped Davey on the shoulder and departed. Davey squirmed and went in to bathe.

The Professor turned to Aunt Agatha. "Good-by. I also will look forward to Sunday. '*You, Miss Martin, we are always sure of.*'"

Aunt Agatha watched his back as he strode up the hill, until he had almost reached the top. Then she laughed and ran into the house.

She did come over to see the Professor's roses and have tea. The rose garden was far larger than that at Lavender Hill and the roses were in wonderful condition. The Professor had many rare varieties and was continually adding new ones. She was introduced to Mr. Meeker, who regarded her solemnly and asked, "Gaowin' to rain?"

Aunt Agatha feared it was not. "Need it," he replied mournfully.

She complimented him on the splendid condition of the roses and the neatness of the garden. Mr. Meeker actually smiled, that is, for him it was a smile; on any other countenance it would hardly have been noticeable.

"We do the best we can, me and the Professor," he said. "Takes a lot of work though. Could raise five-six acres of potatoes with less trouble. Wouldn't be quite as pretty though, I guess."

As they walked toward the terrace for tea the Professor said, "I haven't told Mrs. Meeker just what to have because I knew you would enjoy her order taking."

Mrs. Meeker was introduced and beamed on Aunt Agatha. "Sure is nice to get to know your neighbors," she said heartily. "Davey's a great lad. And to think of his Ma being Garda Garrison! I can't hardly take it in—her having a home right here over the hill. You know, I haven't missed a Garda Garrison picture since there was any. Even Meeker—they're the only pictures I can ever get him to take me to." Remembering her duties, she asked, "Well, folks, what'll it be?"

Aunt Agatha decided on tea, with lemon, please. The Professor would have tea but with cream; Davey ginger ale.

"Okay." Mrs. Meeker recited, "One oolong sour, one with cow, and a ginger for Davey. Be right with you."

She disappeared, and Aunt Agatha said, "She's a darling soul, Professor, you don't realize how fortunate you are. And so *clean!*"

Indeed, china, linen, glass, and silver fairly sparkled. A huge vase of roses graced the table. The chairs, even the stones of the terrace, looked newly scrubbed.

"I do indeed realize my good fortune," the Professor said. "She is truly a treasure. If cleanliness ranks next to godliness, Emmy should rate high among the very top angels. Meeker too—he is the soul of integrity, industry, and sobriety. He gets drunk only three times a year: Christmas, the Fourth of July, and Labor Day. I think it shows a splendid balance; Christmas for religion, the Fourth for patriotism, and Labor Day for social consciousness. They're very mild binges at that. The rest of the year he touches nothing stronger than coffee, and Emmy's coffee is not very strong."

As the summer passed along Aunt Agatha often strolled over in the late afternoon to walk home with Davey. At

Lavender Hill there was a large chest filled with signed photographs of Garda Garrison. She picked out two and presented them to the Meekers, which practically disrupted the Professor's household for a week. Mrs. Meeker's adoration of Aunt Agatha grew nearly to equal hers for Garda Garrison, and Meeker smiled so often that it became almost a habit, instead of an event, as formerly.

More and more often the Professor dropped over to Lavender Hill; sometimes for tea, sometimes dinner, sometimes just to sit in the cool of the evening.

Occasionally the Reverend Beasley was there. He, it seemed, had embarked on a small crusade to bring religion to the Carter clan, with remarkable lack of success.

"A pretty hopeless task, I would say," the Professor remarked.

"The thornier the vineyard, the dearer the fruit," the Reverend said sadly. "The old gentleman called Uncle Eppa is the only one with whom I have made any appreciable progress. There are times when he really seems to begin to see the light."

"He always gets gloomy after one of those warm beer and red wine benders," Davey said. "I guess those are the times. He's crazy anyway."

"*Darling!*" Aunt Agatha reproved.

12. The Forsyth

Dropping into the study one morning not long after the fire, Davey found the Professor surrounded by packing material and fondling a newly arrived gun. "Well, my boy," he said, beaming, "take a look at that—the famous Forsyth."

It was unlike any pistol that Davey had ever seen. There were two barrels, one above the other, two locks and hammers. The firing mechanism was completely strange.

"One of the first, perhaps the very first, percussion arm," the Professor explained. "Not fired by a cap—that came later. In this one a small pellet of detonating powder is dropped into the touch-hole. Then this pin on the hammer explodes the pellet. One of the most remarkable features is this little magazine which holds a supply of pellets and drops them one at a time into the touch-hole." He demonstrated the mechanism to Davey.

"Are we going to test it?" Davey asked.

"Not with a heavy load. It's too valuable historically to take any chances with. What's more, I'd hate to have three thousand dollars blow up in my face."

Davey whistled. "Is that what it cost?"

"It is," the Professor admitted a bit sheepishly. "Even Cousin Harold viewed the price with raised eyebrows. That is, if one can raise eyebrows in a letter."

The Professor had had a beautifully polished mahogany case made for his treasure. It was lined with black velvet and had a glass-top. All day the case reposed on the Professor's desk in a place of honor, while he and Davey took turns examining the new gun.

"It's not as beautiful as many of the other guns," the Professor admitted, "although the gold inlay and the engraving are very handsome, but think of its historical importance. It spelled the doom of the flintlock, and it was only a short step from this to the metallic cartridge, which completely revolutionized all firearms.

"And to think that it was invented by a reverend. Yes, the Reverend Alexander John Forsyth of Belkelvie, Scotland, has a lot to answer for in the development of lethal weapons. I must kid Beasley a bit about that."

Sometime during the afternoon the quiet was broken by the unpleasantly familiar popping of a tractor and raucous voices.

"Well," said the Professor, "apparently Bert has at last seen fit to cut the hay. He's only about two months late, which is doing pretty well for him. Of course the hay is completely dried up now, but I suppose he'll use it."

They could hear Mr. Meeker's nasal twang. "What you gaowin' to use that stuff for—beddin'?"

"Nope," Bert bawled, "they'll eat it, come winter. Either that or snowballs." They heard Uncle Eppa's cackle and Sonny Boy's sneering laugh.

"I wonder how the Reverend is making out with the Carter tribe." The Professor grinned. "He certainly has picked himself a thorny vineyard."

"And pretty rotten fruit," Davey said.

Davey didn't go over the next day. The Professor was in New York but was coming to Lavender Hill for dinner.

"Did you get any new guns?" Davey asked when he arrived.

"No indeed. The Forsyth will have to do me for some time. I won't dare face Cousin Harold for at least two months. I did order a few roses though."

After dinner he produced some catalogues and showed Aunt Agatha the new roses. He had also ordered a few for her. Of course she protested slightly, but she examined the colored photographs with delight.

"The pictures always look a bit better," he said, "but I've seen these in the flesh and they're all pretty swell."

"The rose has but a summer reign," Davey declaimed. *"The daisy never dies."*

"Darling!" Aunt Agatha reproved, but she did not dare catch the Professor's eye.

Next morning when Davey dropped in he found Lieutenant Corrigan settled in one of the deep chairs. He was in uniform today, but his hat lay on the couch, and the glasses, in spite of the uniform, gave him his usual professional appearance. He smiled pleasantly at Davey.

The Professor sat at his desk, looking rather grim.

"I might as well tell you at once, Davey," he said crisply, "the Forsyth has been stolen."

"The Forsyth!" Davey gasped.

"Yes, the Forsyth," the Professor said. "*You* are under suspicion. McKinley, the Meekers, the Carter outfit are all under suspicion; in fact, according to the Lieutenant's reasoning, I may even have stolen it myself."

"You could have—" Lieutenant Corrigan laughed quietly— "in your sleep. It's been done." He placed his fingertips together and looked out at the sky. "You see, it's this way, Davey."

He began to review the facts, as much, apparently, for his own benefit as for Davey's.

"The Professor was in New York all day yesterday. When he got home he bathed, dressed, and went over to your house for dinner. When he came back he went right up to bed. He hadn't been in the study here any time yesterday or last night.

And all that time the door was either open or unlocked. Mrs. Meeker remembers closing it yesterday evening but doesn't remember whether she locked it or not. Probably not, because it was not locked this morning."

"We never lock doors here," the Professor began.

"I know, I know," the Lieutenant interrupted mildly. "That's one of those queer forms of idiocy that some people take pride in. But anyway, as I was saying, anyone could have walked in any time yesterday or last night and taken this gun.

"It could have been you, Davey. You're crazy about guns and you're always over here. It could have been the Meekers; they know how valuable it is. It could have been one of those Carters. It could have been your hired man; he comes over sometimes to talk to Meeker about roses."

"It *could* have been Miss Martin," the Professor interposed rather irritably, "Or my Cousin Harold, or the Reverend Beasley, or Joe Stalin—"

"Could be," the Lieutenant agreed pleasantly. "But getting down to facts, it would be one of two types. Either someone who knew a lot about old guns and realized this one's value, or some light-fingered idiot who just picked up the first thing that caught his eye.

"The only one around who fits the first type is Davey here. You didn't do it, did you, Davey?" His voice was kind and soft as ever, but his look was intent. Davey suddenly realized how terrible it would be to be really guilty of something and try to face those searching blue eyes. "You didn't, did you, Davey?" the Lieutenant repeated softly.

"No, I didn't, I really didn't," Davey answered simply. "How could I?"

The Lieutenant leaned back and resumed his contemplation of the sky.

"Then it's some dope who just couldn't resist picking something up. It wouldn't be a professional, because what could anyone do with a thing like that?"

"That's what I've been saying," the Professor said. "It's too well known. No collector or dealer would touch it. No pawnbroker would give more than a couple of dollars on it—to him it would just be another old gun. Why, you might just as well try to get rid of the Statue of Liberty!"

"Then there's the hired man, McKinley," the Lieutenant mused.

"He was in the garden all day," Davey protested. "I was with him almost all the time until he went home at four-thirty. I guess he went straight home, he usually does. His wife could tell you."

"Temporarily we can cross him off," the Lieutenant said, "and the Meekers—temporarily. Then there is the Carter crew."

"Now at last you're getting warm," the Professor exclaimed. "A good-for-nothing lot if I ever saw one. There's the old man, Uncle Eppa, crazy as a coot. There's Bert, hasn't enough brains or ambition to—"

But Davey already knew. He had known all along.

For the moment he had stepped into the study, above the smell of the Lieutenant's uniform and his saddle-soaped belt and holster, above the smell of guns, powder, gun grease, oil, and polish, he had, faintly but clearly, smelled Sonny Boy.

Always, to Davey, every individual had his, or her, distinctive odor, never strong, seldom unpleasant, but perfectly distinctive. And now all morning, with a steadily increasing depression, he had been smelling Sonny Boy. His mind was in a turmoil. He could hardly concentrate on what the Professor and the Lieutenant were saying.

"Of course we're pretty well agreed," the Lieutenant said, "that it was one of them. But which one? I could shake it out of that little rat in two minutes, but that would never do. That would be police brutality."

He leaned back in his chair and gazed at the sky a while, then turned to Davey. "As I figure it, it was this way. The Professor was away. Mrs. Meeker was out in the kitchen, sewing and listening to the radio. Meeker was way down there in the vegetable garden most of the day. They went to bed about eight o'clock, an old Maine custom. Sometime during the day or the evening or night, somebody wandered or sneaked into the study here.

"The first thing that would catch his eye was this gun in its fancy case, right up here on the desk. So he lifted it. He'd been reading detective stories and thought he knew all the answers, so he was careful to take his handkerchief and wipe off any fingerprints from the case and from the doorknob. We've tried them.

"But of course he wasn't as smart as he thought he was. They never are. The dope dropped his handkerchief right there beside the steps on the terrace. You might take a smell of it."

The Professor pointed to a dirty grayish cloth on his desk. "A nauseating rag," he said distastefully. "Even I can smell it, but I couldn't identify it."

Davey forced himself to go over and sniff at it, but it wasn't necessary. As clearly as though Sonny Boy were in the room, he could smell him. There was the smell of the sweaty blue jeans, the broad leather belt, the odor of the barn—cows, hay, manure. It was unmistakable. Both the Professor and the Lieutenant were watching him intently, but he couldn't speak. He took another long sniff, to gain a few seconds.

In those seconds there flashed through his mind a whole series of pictures. He and Sonny Boy down in the swimming hole—Sonny Boy had taught him to swim. He and Sonny Boy skating and Sonny Boy building a fire to warm their feet and roast potatoes. They were hunting woodchucks, and Sonny Boy generously offered him the first shot. He'd been awfully decent in those days. Older, stronger, more skilled in everything than Davey, always helping him, always teaching him. . . . Then he saw Sonny Boy under the glaring lights at the Police Barracks, surrounded by cops. Just as the Professor had described it—trapped, terrified, blustering, squirming, sweating, lying—and finally wilting before those icy blue eyes of Lieutenant Corrigan.

He couldn't do it. He'd have to work it out some other way. For the first time in his life Davey lied.

He took a final sniff. "It smells," he said, "exactly like one of the taverns down town. I wouldn't know which one, they all smell about the same from the sidewalk. It must be someone who spends a lot of time in the taverns."

The Lieutenant's eyes showed a flicker of disappointment. "Well, I guess that crosses off Sonny Boy," he said. "He's not quite old enough for the taverns—yet."

"What about Uncle Eppa and that wine-beer mixture of his?" the Professor suggested. "That ought to put a tavern smell even on his shoes."

"No, that's different," Davey smiled. "It's a little the same but sourer."

"Well, there we are." The Lieutenant sighed. "Nowhere." He gathered up his hat. "Sorry, Professor. Of course we'll check the pawnshops and I'll have one of the boys do a little sitting around in the taverns, but it doesn't look too promising. Don't let it get noised around or in the papers. Whoever has it might get scared and throw it down the well or in the river."

"That's what upsets me," the Professor said. "It isn't the money, the thing's insured anyway. But to think that one of the most historically important guns in the world is in the hands of some halfwit who, as you say, may throw it in the river or bury it under a manure pile is maddening."

13. "You've Got to Give It Back, Clyde"

As Davey walked home across the fields for lunch the tumult in his mind steadied down. He knew what he had to do.

Both Rose and Aunt Agatha noticed his quietness at lunch. Aunt Agatha attributed it to the walls of the stomach, Rose to Love. Any behavior out of the ordinary she always attributed to Love.

After lunch Davey got out his bicycle and rode down the drive. He turned left onto the black road and coasted down the hill. He crossed the bridge and pedaled steadily across the flats. Finally he turned down a dirt road, crossed another bridge, and rode into the Carter place.

It presented a sad but perfect picture of beauty and elegance gone to ruin. The lovely proportions and detail of the old house were still present but fast disappearing. The rotting roof was patched here and there with tin or tarpaper. The small-paned, delicately mullioned windows had much of their glass replaced by rags or cardboard. From the kitchen window a rusty stovepipe stuck out at a crazy angle.

Great maples shaded what had been the lawn but was now a graveyard for discarded farm equipment. Two or three dirty children scuttled into the house at his approach.

Davey rode on out to the barnyard. The new cow barn, stark and unpainted, was already showing signs of neglect; broken windows, rotting sills, sagging doors. There, as he had hoped, he found Sonny Boy, cleaning out the cow stalls.

"Hiya, kid," Sonny Boy called. His voice was hard with suspicion. As Davey approached a strange opaque film seemed to settle over Sonny Boy's dark eyes. They fixed, not on Davey's face, but on a point just above his left shoulder.

"Clyde," Davey said, "you've got to give it back."

"Give what back?" Sonny Boy said through tight lips. "What're you talkin' about?"

"You know. Professor Benton's gun. You've *got* to, Clyde.

It's no good to you; you can't sell it, and it may get you in a lot of trouble."

Sonny Boy's eyes became more opaque and narrowed still more. "You're crazy," he sneered, "I've never seen any gun."

"Clyde," Davey almost begged, "this is really important. It's one of the rarest guns in the world. It isn't like my field glass and McKinley's wallet. I know you took those too—I smelled them on you. But—"

He saw Sonny Boy's nostrils flare, his eyes close to slits. Then there was a blinding red explosion. He staggered and tried to put up his guard, but he was no match for Sonny Boy, he never had been. There was another crashing blow and the sickening taste of blood. Another in the pit of the stomach took his wind and doubled him over. A great blinding flare of red, and through his one good eye he saw the end of the barn describe a rising arc. The ground heaved up and struck him. He could feel the gravel grind into his face.

He started to struggle to his feet and was met by another smash—this one on the mouth—and went down again.

Once more he managed to stagger to his feet and face Sonny Boy. Sonny Boy's eyes were still slits. His hair hung in black streaks over his forehead. He was breathing hard through quivering nostrils. "Got enough," he grated, "or do you want some more?"

Davey shook his head and wiped the blood from his mouth. His lips were split and swollen, making it hard to talk. One eye was completely closed.

RL

"You've got to give it back, Clyde," he said doggedly. "You dropped your handkerchief and the police have got it. I could smell it, but I wouldn't tell them—yet. You've got to give it back."

Sonny Boy's hand slid into a pocket and came out with a pocketknife. He pressed a button, and a wicked-looking blade sprang out. His eyes were still fixed above Davey's shoulder.

"Listen, you snooty little rich creep," he breathed. "You blab one word to the cops and I'll kill you. I'll cut your guts out."

For a moment Davey thought he was going to, right then, and didn't much care. He stumbled over and picked up his bicycle.

"You've *got* to give it back, Clyde," he repeated.

He mounted and coasted a wobbly course down to the road. When he reached the bridge he got off, went down to the brook, and plunged his head into the cool water. He mopped at his nose with his wet handkerchief and the bleeding slowly lessened. He gingerly touched his face, which had an unfamiliar, lumpy contour. His left eye was tightly closed, one front tooth felt loose. His shirt was a hopeless mess; he rolled it up and hid it in the bushes.

He pedaled wearily across the flats, speeding cars honking at his erratic course. He couldn't make the hill, he had to dismount and trudge up, pushing his bicycle. He dropped it by the garage, hoping to get up to his room unobserved.

But in the back hall he met Rose. She took one horrified

look. "My baby!" she wailed, "what they done to you?" She wrapped him in her arms and then Davey cried a little. The tears stung his swollen eye.

"It's all right," he finally managed to say. "I just got in a fight and got licked."

Rose wisely asked no more questions but rushed him upstairs. While he soaked in a boiling hot bath she fetched liniments and salves. She bathed his battered face with witch hazel, rubbed his cut lips with salve. Her fingers gently probed the swollen eye.

"Just a shiner," she pronounced, "but it shore is a lollapalooza. You lie down on your bed now, whilst I fetch a piece of beef for it. Good thing your Aunt Agtha ain't home."

She returned shortly with a slab of raw beef and placed it gently on the bad eye. "There now, honey," she said, "just you lie here awhile and rest yo'self." She stroked his forehead softly.

Davey fell asleep immediately and slept soundly for an hour or so. When he waked most of the soreness and pain were eased. He felt wonderfully relaxed. He removed the slab of beef and looked at himself in the mirror. Had it not been so painful he would have laughed. The bad eye was slightly open now, but the swelling was a deep blue, edged with reddish purple. His lips and nose were red and swollen, there were various lumps, and his forehead was scraped by gravel. He washed his face again, very gingerly, combed his hair, put on clean clothes, and went downstairs, carrying the beef.

"Thanks, Rose," he said, "you certainly are a grand doctor. I feel fine now."

Rose surveyed him critically. "You look better," she admitted, "but you certainly ain't pretty. Better let me tell your Aunt Agtha when she come home. Prepare her like."

Davey wandered out to the terrace. He didn't want any more questions. But almost immediately he was confronted by McKinley. Evidently Rose had been talking.

McKinley looked seven feet tall. His face was set like graven basalt, his eyes fastened stonily on the horizon.

"Mist' Davey," he demanded, "who done you this way?"

"Oh, it's all right." Davey managed a laugh. "I just got in a little fight and got licked."

"That weren't no fight," McKinley said. "That were a beatin'." His hands grasped Davey's shoulders, almost lifting him from the ground. His fingers were like steel hooks.

"Mist' Davey," he repeated, *"who done you this way?"*

"I told you," Davey cried. "Leave me alone." The pain brought tears to his eyes. "You're hurting me."

McKinley's grip relaxed. His great hands flexed and then clenched into knotted lumps. The muscles of his forearms rose in hard ridges. His set face still looked toward the horizon.

"I'll find 'em out," he said softly. "I'll find 'em out and hunt 'em down. Can't nobody do my folks this way."

He turned abruptly and stalked toward the old Ford.

14. A Pillar of Fire by Night

Rose had met Aunt Agatha and tactfully prepared her for the shock of Davey's appearance. Also, she had quite evidently stressed the fact that he did not want to be questioned. For although Aunt Agatha had wept copiously at the sight of his injuries and made a great fuss over him, she did not make a

129

single query as to what had happened, or why, or how. For all of which Davey was deeply grateful.

Now, next morning, he was sitting on the terrace doing nothing special. The bad eye had changed from purplish blue to greenish, but the swelling had gone down a great deal and he could see pretty well with it. The other injuries were healing rapidly. It wasn't even painful to smile.

About midmorning he became conscious of the Professor's voice. He was talking to Aunt Agatha out in the rose garden.

"Where is my lazy apprentice? A fine faithful lad he is! I shall cut his yearly wage to one shilling sixpence."

He approached the terrace and then stopped, aghast at Davey's battered countenance. "Good grief!" he exclaimed. "What have you tangled with?"

"Oh, I just got in a fight and got licked," Davey said.

"With how many wildcats?" the Professor demanded. "Or was it only a Mack truck?"

Davey just laughed. The Professor settled in a chair and hung his legs over the arm. "What I came over to tell you," he said, "is the big news. The Forsyth has been returned."

"Oh, grand," Davey exclaimed. A huge weight seemed to lift from his still-aching head. He relaxed in his chair. "Oh, gee, that's just wonderful!"

The Professor lit his pipe and went on, "There it was this morning on the study doorstep, wrapped in a piece of newspaper, all safe and sound. Meeker tripped over it when he went out to sweep the terrace. Corrigan came by and wanted to test it for fingerprints, but I said why bother? The gun's back and that's all that matters. So he gave us a lecture on the stupidity of leaving things unlocked—a pretty severe one. I'm sure that from now on the Meekers will have me locked out every time I step forth to pluck a rose."

The Professor puffed gently on his pipe, gazing at the pleasant fields and the cloud-dotted sky. Davey felt so relieved and relaxed that he almost dozed.

"Davey," the Professor finally said, "I'm not one to pry or mess in other people's affairs, but even to my dull brain there seems to be a definite connection between recent happenings. The Forsyth is stolen—you get your face battered to a pulp— the Forsyth is returned. Of course, as I say, I don't want to ask unwelcome questions."

"All right, don't." Davey smiled. "The gun's back and that's all that matters."

They sat awhile, enjoying the beautiful morning. Finally the Professor got up to go. "You know," he said, "Corrigan made an odd remark this morning. He said, 'Of course I knew the young Martin lad was lying yesterday about that handkerchief. Decent people don't lie very well.' "

He looked quizzically at Davey, but Davey only smiled.

The Professor rejoined Miss Agatha in the rose garden. "Well," he said, "he certainly took a beating, but he's curing quickly, and he seems in fine spirits now that the gun is returned. The whole thing fits together in my mind pretty well. I didn't try to pry too much, but I would really like to know."

"*I* know," Aunt Agatha said quietly. "Last night I was worried and went in to see if he was all right. He was sleeping restlessly; he was probably a bit feverish. I sat there awhile and he kept repeating, 'Clyde, you've got to give it back. You've got to give it back, Clyde,' over and over again." Her eyes grew misty.

"Clyde is Sonny Boy's real name. They used to be great friends. Now do you see?"

The Professor plucked a beetle and ground it under his foot. "Well I'll be hanged," he said. "But it's about what I suspected." He smiled wryly. "Greater love hath no man than this, that a man have his face smashed in for his friends. He's a grand boy. I would be tremendously proud to have him as a—nephew."

Aunt Agatha flung herself on Davey and threw her arms around his neck. She kissed the swollen eye and cried all over his lumpy face. "My poor darling," she choked, "are you *sure* you're all right?"

"Of course I'm all right," he answered grumpily. He had been half asleep. "What's the matter with *you?*"

She laughed through her tears. "I don't know. I'm just silly, I guess."

"Well, you'd better find out," Davey chuckled. "Eating lunch in that state will raise heck with your Walls."

Life at Lavender Hill resumed its quiet way. Almost all of the Professor's collection had by now received its annual cleaning. Davey's bruises had all disappeared, except for a faint tinge of blue under the left eye.

McKinley, however, continued to brood. Every time his glance fell on Davey's face his eyes grew somber and sought the horizon. His quiet smile appeared seldom, and he was given to long periods of silence.

Rose commented on it to Aunt Agatha. "That man McKinley worry me," she said. "He mighty broody. Just go gloomin' around all day, sayin' nothin'. I tell him no use acting that way. Mist' Davey all right now. Ain't hardly a mark on him. He forgot all about that beatin'. But McKinley he just look mean and keep saying, 'I'll find 'em out. Can't nobody do my folks that way.'

"I hope he never do, 'cause he liable to do somethin' ugly. Funny thing, but when a quiet, gentle man like him get good and mad they's the dangerousest kind there is."

The Professor's visits became more frequent, and Aunt Agatha's afternoon strolls usually ended at the Professor's study or his rose garden. The Reverend Beasley seldom appeared nowadays, and Aunt Agatha, feeling a little bad about it, invited him to dinner.

Of course the Professor had been asked too, and now, after

dinner, they sat in the twilight on the terrace. McKinley, who had stayed to serve dinner, brought the coffee.

"Thank you, McKinley," Aunt Agatha said. "You'd better run along home now. Rose will get the tray."

"Thank you, Miss Agtha," he replied somberly. "Good night to you all." His white coat faded into the darkness.

"Give my best to Ulysses David Calhoun," the Professor called.

The Reverend discoursed at some length on the subject of Uncle Eppa, with whom he now felt he had made definite progress.

"I do believe," he said, "that I may eventually make a decent Christian of him. At times his repentance is so deep as to be almost alarming."

Davey was about to offer a comment, but a quick glance from Aunt Agatha cut it off.

The Professor gently teased the Reverend a bit about the Reverend Forsyth and his invention. "He has a lot to answer for," said the Professor. "All our modern deadly weapons stem from his idea. The odd thing, too, was that it was developed to help in hunting game at night. The flash of a flintlock pan usually startled the prey, so in order to avoid this the Reverend Forsyth invented his new percussion method.

"One hesitates to bring up the point, but of course at that time the only people who hunted at night were poachers. I have always wondered if perhaps the Reverend, with a large family to feed—they always had large families—and an infinitesimal salary—this was Scotland, remember—might not have been driven to—"

"Oh, Professor!" Aunt Agatha laughed. "You're just making a lot of that up." She leaned back in her chair and breathed the soft air. "What a lovely evening," she sighed, "and we're going to have a beautiful moonrise."

"Moonrise?" the Professor said. "Why, there's no moon until the twentieth." He looked across the rolling countryside and at the glow behind the hills to the east. He sprang to his feet. "That's no moon!"

At that instant the evening quiet was shattered by the village siren. "*This* time we go," he exclaimed.

They all ran for Miss Agatha's car. Davey, the Professor, and Aunt Agatha crowded into the front seat; the Reverend, who was somewhat slower, clambered into the back.

They swept down the drive, and as they turned into the road they could hear the howling sirens of the engines roaring out from the village. Lots of cars were heading for the glow, but they were well ahead of most of them. Aunt Agatha, who was a splendid driver, zoomed down the hill, crossed the bridge, and sped across the flats.

"By George, it's the Carter place!" the Professor shouted. "I'm sure it is."

A sudden cold fear gripped Davey. He remembered that set, brooding look on McKinley's face, the ever-repeated, "I'll find 'em out." He remembered Rose's ominous warning, "Them quiet ones is the dangerousest." This was the route that McKinley took on his way home. There had been just about time. . . .

They turned into the dirt road, which was already choking with dust.

"It's the barn," the Professor exclaimed.

They clattered over the little bridge, and suddenly Miss Agatha jammed on the brakes and swerved off the road into the bushes. She pulled on the emergency brake. "I can't," she gasped. "The cows—it would be too ghastly. Thirty-six cows locked in their stanchions. We *can't* go."

Davey, standing on the seat, peered through the dust. "The cows are all right," he announced. "They're all out. They're down in the corner of the pasture. Let's go."

Two fire engines from the village thundered past and up the Carter drive, followed by a stream of cars. It was impossible to get back on the road, so they left the car and scrambled through the bushes and up the hill. A small knoll between the house and the barn gave a good viewpoint.

The roaring barn lit up the whole scene with a glare like orange daylight. The barn was not far from the brook, and already the engines had spread their hoses and were beginning to pump. The streams, however, had little effect on the conflagration; it was clear that the best the firemen could do would be to keep the fire from spreading to the other buildings and the fields. The roads were now choked with cars, their headlights shining dimly through dust clouds. More people kept arriving and spreading over the field. The cows were still huddled in the far corner of the pasture. A few cropped grass, but most of them gazed with round solemn eyes at the fire.

Not far away a knot of men was gathered, talking violently. Davey recognized Chief Dolan, Bert, and Sonny Boy. The rest were a rough-looking crew of Carter relatives and friends.

"It was set, I tell you!" Bert kept bawling. "The whole place stunk of gasoline. Somebody set it!"

Davey grew cold.

"How come the cows got out?" Chief Dolan asked.

"How'd I know how they got out?" Bert shouted. "We were inside eatin' supper, I tell you. When we got out here the cows were all out. Whoever set it afire let 'em out first. I tell you it stunk of gasoline—anybody could smell it."

"Barn insured?" the Chief inquired.

" 'Course it ain't," Bert yelled. "How can a poor man like me buy insurance? It's all I got and it's ruined me." He was blubbering with rage.

With horror Davey suddenly became aware that McKinley was standing beside them.

"Evening, Miss Agtha," he said politely. "Evening, Professor. Evening Reverent—Mist' Davey." Davey could not bring himself to speak. McKinley gazed into the flames with that strange look of rapt excitement which always gripped him at fires.

They heard Sonny Boy's shrill voice. "It's that hired man of the Martins, I tell you. I seen his car parked down by the river. He's the one set it!"

"I saw it too," one of the men shouted excitedly. "What's more, I saw him lugging a five-gallon gasoline can down the road. There he is now. Let's get him!"

As they advanced toward the knoll Aunt Agatha drew close to McKinley. He had heard nothing, he was too engrossed in the fire. Now he turned mildly inquiring eyes on the approaching crowd. Several had snatched up clubs, pick handles, stones. More voices took up the cry, "Let's get him!"

The Professor stepped out briskly to meet them and faced Bert.

"Don't be an ass," he snapped. "Why would he come back here and show himself if he'd fired your barn? Why would he let out your cows if he wanted to ruin you? Why would he burn your silly barn anyway?"

Chief Dolan took a stand beside the Professor, facing the crowd. The Reverend stoutly joined them, the three argued, cajoled, and tried to reason, but the mob was in an ugly mood. Even the more respectable farmers and neighbors became infected; to them barn burning ranked second only to murder.

Someone threw a stone which struck McKinley's temple a glancing blow, but he never noticed. He seemed completely bewildered. A slight trickle of blood ran down his face and he brushed at it absently, as though it were a fly. Aunt Agatha placed herself in front of him, her eyes flashing defiance. Other, more responsible men joined the Professor, forming a barrier before the muttering crowd.

Suddenly Sonny Boy wormed through and faced McKinley. His face was white with venom.

"*He* done it," he screamed. "He done it to get even, because I beat up that dopy little sissy-pants brat! That's why he done it!"

A slow smile of satisfaction spread over McKinley's countenance. He took a step forward, his hands shot out like striking snakes and fastened on Sonny Boy's skinny shoulders. They lifted him clear of the ground.

"*You?*" he murmured softly. "You beat Mist' Davey? *You!*"

Davey and Aunt Agatha struggled and pulled at the rigid arms; they might as well have tugged at the branches of an oak tree. McKinley still wore that happy smile, but his eyes were blank and unseeing. Without loosing their grip the great hands were working relentlessly toward Sonny Boy's throat.

Davey stretched up and with all his strength slapped him across the face—three times.

Slowly, like a sleepwalker coming to consciousness, reason returned to McKinley's eyes. His grip relaxed and Sonny Boy slunk away. McKinley's hand automatically touched his face. His voice was filled with wonder. "Mist' Davey," he said unbelievingly, "Mist' Davey, you struck me!"

Davey was crying with rage and fear. "I'll do it again if you don't behave," he stormed. "You crazy fool, haven't you done enough tonight?"

"Mist' Davey," McKinley, still wondering, protested, "I done nothin'."

One of the Carter women rushed from the house bearing a shotgun and thrust it into Bert's hands. "Bert," she shrilled, "you going to let anybody lay hands on Sonny Boy that way? Go get him!"

Someone else pushed through the crowd, carrying a five-gallon can. He shoved it at Chief Dolan. "There it is," he shouted. "In the back of his car. There's still about a gallon of gas in it."

One of the Carter men hurled an insult at Miss Agatha and there was a sharp smack as the Reverend Beasley's fist landed solidly on his jaw. The man staggered back, for a moment his knees buckled, then he started forward with a roar of rage. Aunt Agatha gasped, but the Reverend's face was grimly eager and his guard looked impressively professional. There was a momentary pause.

"All right, boys," Bert bawled, "what're we waiting for? Let's go." The mob began to surge forward.

At that moment Davey caught the flash of spectacles and a second later saw Lieutenant Corrigan, flanked by two husky officers, plowing a way through the crowd.

The Lieutenant walked unhurriedly up to the threatening muzzle of Bert's shotgun, placed his hand gently on the barrel, and tilted it toward the sky.

"All right," he said quietly, "give to Papa."

Bert's grip relaxed helplessly and he released the gun. The Lieutenant broke it and looked into the unloaded breech. "You *wouldn't* have shells," he said with quiet scorn. "You

wouldn't have anything. Too shiftless and good-for-nothing."
He threw the gun disgustedly on the ground. "Now, what's
this all about?"

There was a clamor of voices. Chief Dolan explained matters to the Lieutenant, pointing several times at the gasoline
can.

The Lieutenant turned to McKinley. "Well, what about it?"
he demanded.

McKinley smiled his disarming smile. "Captain, suh," he
said, "it's this way. Goin' home this evenin', right down here
by the river, my car stop. I look and my gas tank's clean
empty, so I walk back to the gas station on the corner and buy
some gasoline. I only buy one gallon 'cause I ain't only got
twenty-five cents. The gent'man loan me a can to carry it in.
When I get back here I see the fire, so I put the can in the
back of the car and come on up."

A man in a leather jacket stepped out of the crowd. "That's
right, Lieutenant," he said. "I sold him a gallon of gas just a
little while ago. He hadn't hardly time to get back here, let
alone set any fire. That's my can." He picked it up, hefted it
with practiced hand, and peered into the opening. "The full
gallon's still in there."

Davey drew a great breath of relief.

There were sudden cries from the spectators as with a great
crash the barn roof collapsed. A huge geyser of sparks rose
hundreds of feet in the air. The firemen threw a fresh stream
on the roof of the house, while others rushed around with

hand extinguishers, putting out grass fires. The flames rose in a solid column, lighting up the entire countryside. The roar and crackling were terrifying.

At that moment Davey became aware of Uncle Eppa's wild cackle and realized that he had not appeared before. Uncle Eppa advanced toward the small knot on the knoll, screeching crazily. His face, even in the orange glare of the flames, was pasty white, the red semicircle on his forehead stood out lividly. He burst through the crowd and stopped, glaring dramatically at McKinley.

"Don't let *him* get no credit for doing the Lord's work!" he shrieked. "He never set no fire. *I* done it! God told me to! The Reverend set me on the path and I seen the light. The Lord stretched out His hand and lain a curse on these miserable sinners.

"He says rain down fire and brimstone on 'em, them and their blaspheming and lying and stealing. 'Their wickedness burneth as the fire,' He says. 'Woe be unto them that follows not His commands.'

"I lit a pillar of fire to lead 'em the way by night!"

"Shut up, you crazy old fool," Sonny Boy snarled. The flames roared louder, and Uncle Eppa's voice rose to a shriek.

"Crazy am I?" he screeched. "*You're* the crazy one—thinking the Lord won't find you out and smite you down." He cackled wildly. "*You*—the wickedest of the lot. Don't think the Lord don't know about your sins. I've told him about your thieving and lying and stealing. You can hide your stole loot behind the paneling but you can't hide your sins from the eye of the Lord." He shook his skinny finger in Sonny Boy's face. " 'Woe unto them that defiles the house of their fathers.' "

Lieutenant Corrigan nodded toward Sonny Boy. "Take him," he said quietly. One of the officers slipped the thin steel links of his persuader around Sonny Boy's wrist. "All right, bud," he said. "Let's be good now, *if* you want that arm."

The Lieutenant nodded to another officer. "Go along with him and take a look," he said. The two troopers, with Sonny Boy between them, disappeared into the house.

"Reverend," Uncle Eppa cried, "kneel down with me and pray for their wicked souls." With quiet dignity the Reverend Beasley knelt beside him and said a short prayer. Uncle Eppa's wild eyes stared into the flames, his lips fluttering soundlessly.

"Take *him*," the Lieutenant said to two newly arrived troopers. "Book him for arson. Handle him gently, he's crazy as a cockroach. And get a doctor to give him something to quiet him down, or he'll have us awake all night."

The Reverend offered his hand to Aunt Agatha. The knuckles were skinned and swollen. "Good night," he said. "I shall go with him. I feel greatly responsible for all this." He accompanied Uncle Eppa and the troopers to their car.

Sonny Boy's two captors emerged from the house. One of them carried a bulging pillowcase. He spread the loot out on the ground.

"Why, there's my field glass," Davey exclaimed. "And Mc-Kinley's wallet." McKinley's eyes shone. "McK.W.," he said. "My own letters in gold on my wallet come all the way from London, England."

There were many other articles: three small expensive Kodaks, another wallet, a small bronze sundial, a few pieces of silverware, four wristwatches, two pairs of silk stockings, two bracelets, a revolver with a box of ammunition, three pairs of spectacles, and an envelope full of pawntickets.

"A very enterprising young man," the Lieutenant observed, "who never overlooked an opportunity. This ought to clean up a lot of little matters that have been bothering us lately."

Someone spoke from among the bystanders. "Has one of those Kodaks got an 'A.H.C.' on the case? If it has it's mine. It disappeared about a month ago, when the Carters were cutting our hay."

"Identify it and get it at the barracks tomorrow," the Lieutenant said. "All right, boys, take him and the stuff away." He turned to Aunt Agatha, "Miss Martin, could you spare a cup of coffee for a tired old man? In fact, I think we could all do with one."

"Yes indeed." She laughed. "I could do with three of them myself."

He turned to McKinley. "Williams, suppose you put that gallon of gas in your tank and run up and ask Miss Martin's cook to brew about a gallon of coffee—strong. And don't forget to give that can back to the gas station man. He did you a good turn."

Two troopers who had been directing traffic came up for further orders. "Just stick around," the Lieutenant said. "See if Dolan wants anything, and pick me up at Miss Martin's in about half an hour."

The barn had pretty well burned itself out now. Most of the crowd had left. The cars along the road had untangled themselves and gone away. They went down and got in Aunt Agatha's car. "Professor," she said, "would you mind driving? It's silly, but I feel a little shaky."

The Professor took the wheel, and she leaned back wearily against the cushions. Davey and the Lieutenant got in the back seat.

"Mr. Corrigan," Davey said, "I'm sorry I lied to you that day about the handkerchief."

"You made a pretty poor job of it." The Lieutenant chuckled. "I don't imagine you've had much practice."

"I guess I haven't," Davey admitted. "I think that was my first try."

"Well, see that you don't lose your amateur standing." The Lieutenant smiled.

McKinley, in a fresh white coat, greeted them. A table was set on the terrace, and Rose appeared with a huge steaming urn of coffee.

Aunt Agatha relaxed in her chair and sipped her coffee. "I'm worried about the poor cows," she sighed. "Their home is gone. And poor Bert too. He's *so* good-for-nothing, but pathetic somehow."

"The cows will be all right," the Professor said. "It's a beautiful warm night. They'll do a lot of bawling though. As for Bert, it's probably the best thing that could have happened to him. He will have to sell his cows and take a regular job. He's perfectly capable and ought to make excellent wages—as long as he doesn't have to think."

"Golly," Davey said, "but doesn't the Reverend pack a wallop? I'd hate to get one of those on the jaw."

"He does that," the Lieutenant agreed. "Too bad he didn't try it on some of that Carter crew in the first place instead of prayer. Not that I don't believe in it, mind you, but sometimes a good right swing works a lot faster."

He poured himself another cup of coffee, leaned back in his chair, and sighed. "I hope you'll excuse me for forcing myself on you this way, Miss Martin," he said, "but I always feel let down when I have to face the dreary business.

"There's the old man, crazy as a coot, of course, but arson's a serious charge. We'll have to get some sort of statement and probably have to listen to him rave all night. It isn't fun.

"Then there's the young one, and that's the really tough part. Every time I have to take one of that age I always think, 'There but for the grace of something-or-other goes one of my two.' Of course they're good kids and he's a really bad egg, but it's wearing just the same. He's only fifteen, so he won't get anything much, a few weeks or months in a corrective school. Then he gets out and goes on to bigger and better things. Eventually he'll be Sonny Boy Carter, a small-time Public Enemy. May end up in a gutter, full of holes. Maybe will have killed a couple of decent cops first, cops with families, like me. He's rotten."

"But, Lieutenant," Aunt Agatha asked, "isn't it a matter of early environment and education and lack of opportunity? Couldn't something have been done?"

Lieutenant Corrigan finished his coffee and poured another cup. "That's what they say, Miss Martin, and it sounds good—in the magazines. All I know is what really goes on.

"Why, look, here's Webber, Sergeant, going to get my job when I retire. He came out of a home that would make the Carters' look like a young ladies' finishing school. He's one of the best men on the force. Then there's Daley, you saw tonight. Father was a drunken ex-prizefighter. Never saw his mother—luckily. Didn't have any more opportunity than a stray alley cat, an early environment that would give you nightmares. Worked his way through school, well educated, steady as a rock. Has a fine wife and a nice kid and a swell little house. He'll be a sergeant soon.

"And then look at these kids on our blotter. A whole string of them. A lot of them out of first families; fine home life, all the education and opportunities in the world. And what does the blotter read? Car stealing, driving while drunk, theft, vandalism, malicious mischief, and worse—oh, much worse. You'd be surprised."

The blinking red lights of a police car came up the drive, and he reached for his hat. He took off his glasses and passed his hand over his tired eyes.

"My own theory is that there's a bad egg in almost every setting and a vicious pup in every so many litters. Of course I know it isn't very scientific, but I've been around a long time and I've seen a lot—too much I guess.

"Good night, Miss Martin. Thanks a lot for the coffee, and for letting me blow off steam. It's a big help sometimes. Come over to the barracks tomorrow, son, and collect your field glass."

In silence they watched the Lieutenant's solid back as he plodded down the walk. "He's due to retire soon," the Professor said. "I hope he does; this thing is getting him down."

Davey heard the sputtering of the old Ford and ran out to tell McKinley good night. McKinley's face wore its old placid smile.

"Good night, McKinley," Davey said, "I'm awfully sorry I hit you."

"That's all right," McKinley chuckled. "Reckon you was worried. Reckon you thought maybe *I* set that barn afire. I couldn't do nothing like that, Mist' Davey, you ought to know that. Much as I do enjoy a good fire."

"Have you got enough gas to get home on?" Davey asked. "One gallon isn't very much."

"Plenty." McKinley laughed. "Professor Benton given me a dollar, and that nice *police* gent'man given me a dollar, and

Miss Agtha given me two dollars. I'm going to get me ten gallons all at one time and leave the can with that service station man. He shore was kindly."

On the terrace Aunt Agatha sighed. "The Lieutenant's talk depresses me," she said. "Davey means *so* much. I have tried to do everything I could, but it *is* a terrible responsibility. Sometimes, especially when I hear things like that, I can't help feeling frightened."

"Don't worry," the Professor said gently. "Davey's swell. He's definitely *not* the bad egg in the setting or the vicious pup in the litter. And he's got everything—except a good old solid, rather unexciting uncle. I would like, ever so much, to nominate myself for the post."

At that moment Davey returned, and the Professor bade them good night.

Aunt Agatha and Davey carried the coffee things out to the kitchen.

"Well, it's been quite an evening." Davey yawned. "I'm sleepy."

Aunt Agatha hugged him and kissed the still slightly blackened eye. To Davey she seemed rather flighty. "You're going to be the very *best* egg in the setting and the very *best* pup in the litter, aren't you, darling?" she asked eagerly.

He didn't quite know what she meant, but he laughed and said, "I guess I'm bound to be. After all, I'm the only one."

15. Your Full and Free Consent

Davey had not looked forward to the return to school with any great enthusiasm, but now that he was back at Brewster and settled down, he was rather enjoying it.

Their old room smelled familiar and homy. It was fun seeing Skinny and Goofer Wallace and all the rest. Goofer's

151

latest passion was collecting sea shells, at which he had spent most of the summer. He talked learnedly of "univalves" and "bivalves," and referred to himself as a "conchologist."

Skinny had had a wonderful summer at the Cape. He pointed out that Davey had missed a great deal by not coming to visit. Skinny had played a lot of tennis and had placed fifth in the Junior Juniors' Tournament. He had had a small sailboat which ranked ninth in the Rainbow Fleet. He had acquired a magnificent tan and a splendid vocabulary of nautical phrases.

Skinny didn't think that Davey had had much of a summer. He couldn't imagine its being any fun to play around with a professor. When he learned that it was Professor Benton, of the Latin grammar, he felt that Davey was a little touched in the head. As for pitching hay, shooting woodchucks, or polishing guns all day—that was not at all Skinny's idea of a good time.

Of course Davey missed Aunt Agatha, the Professor, Rose, and McKinley, but not too much. The pistol the Curator had given him hung in the place of honor over the fireplace, lending a certain air of distinction to the room. Sometimes if Davey woke early he would catch the pleasant odor of oil and polish. At those moments he would be really homesick for Lavender Hill.

One afternoon Skinny brought up two letters for Davey. He held them behind his back. "Who're they from, Smeller?" he demanded. "A nickel on it."

Davey was clearly aware of Aunt Agatha's aroma of lavender and of a medley of gun grease, polish, and tobacco.

"Aunt Agatha and Professor Benton," Davey answered promptly.

Skinny tossed them on the table and produced a nickel. "You certainly haven't lost your schnozzle power," he said ruefully.

Davey opened Aunt Agatha's letter first.

"Darlingest," it read. "I have great news to tell you and have spent most of the afternoon thinking how to do it with tact and skill. I do not seem to have much of either, and the more I thought the more confused I became. So perhaps I had best just be direct.

"Professor Benton has asked me to marry him! There, it's out!

"I have accepted, but on one condition only. Which is that you give your full and free consent, and your blessing. I am sure we would be very happy, but I could never be anything but miserable if you did not approve completely, in fact, were not really enthusiastic.

"So, darling, do think it over most carefully, and do answer me with complete frankness.

"We are planning, if you consent, to be married at Christmas time, during your holidays.

"And still more exciting news. John and Garda have written that they will be home for Christmas! It should be quite an occasion! They are closing the new play in November and bringing it to New York, where it will open in January, so it does seem that they may make a real stay at Lavender Hill. And I suppose that will mean another wristwatch in January!

"And now for other items. Uncle Eppa was found mildly insane and sent to the State Institution. At least the poor creature will, for once, be well fed and taken care of.

"Sonny Boy, as you know, was sent to the Corrective Farm for a short time. Immediately after his release he and his car disappeared. Bert, I understand, has received a picture post-card from Kansas City. Sonny Boy is heading for Hollywood, where he feels there are more opportunities. For just what, he did not state.

"Bert himself, as Professor Benton predicted, sold his cows and now has a good position with the Brass Company. He looks most prosperous and, for the first time in my memory, clean and shaved.

"And Lieutenant Corrigan's retirement papers have at last come through. The dear soul will have a good pension and, of all things, is going to raise Great Danes! He has promised us, as a wedding present, the very best pup of the very first litter.

"Rose, of course, sends her love. She is in ecstasy at the thought of Garda's return. And McKinley says to tell you that it is fortunate that the blue coat John gave him is double-breasted, for now he has *two* wallets for Sunday.

"Darling, do tell me fully and frankly exactly how you feel

about this step. And, of course, you will know how eagerly I await your answer. So do, please, make it soon."

Davey tore open the Professor's letter. It was somewhat shorter and read: "Dear Davey: Without beating around the bush let me announce my momentous news. Your dear Aunt Agatha has done me the great honor of accepting my proposal of marriage. She has written you, I know, and we hope our letters will reach you at the same time.

"As you know, this acceptance is only conditional, depending on your full approval and consent. I shall not attempt to influence you in any manner. You have seen enough of me and my ways to form your own opinion as to whether or not I would make a possible uncle. Of course I cannot begin to express how unbelievably happy your aunt's decision has made me. Yours, if favorable, will cause my cup to run over.

"You will be glad to know, I am sure, that Corrigan has at last been retired. Of course, at the moment, he seems a bit lost; he cannot keep away from the Barracks and visits me quite frequently. I was deeply touched when, on the day his retirement became official, he presented me with his revolver, which he has carried for twenty-odd years, for my collection! It is the only modern gun in the collection and neither particularly handsome or historical, but I shall treasure it greatly.

"You cannot imagine how much good this change has done the man already. He looks ten years younger, is enthusiastically starting to raise Great Danes, and swears that he will never read another newspaper or listen to the radio news as long as he lives.

"And speaking of newspapers, the *Times* recently ran a series of articles gently exposing the famous Dr. Hubert, who wrote *The Walls of Health*. It seems that he was a bit of a charlatan and his theories complete balderdash. I am afraid it was a slight blow to your aunt, but she took it beautifully, as she does everything, threw the book in the trash can, and vowed never to think of, or mention, the Walls again.

"And now, my dear boy, don your robes of judgment and consider well my poor plea. I shall await your decision with the utmost eagerness."

Davey turned hastily to Skinny. "How about lending me that dollar you've got?" he asked.

"What dollar?" Skinny countered warily.

"That dollar bill in your watch pocket. Come on, I can smell it perfectly well."

Skinny sadly extracted the bill and proffered it. "What do you want it for?"

"I've got to send a telegram to Aunt Agatha." Davey laughed happily. "I've got to give my consent for her to marry Professor Benton. Say, how do you spell 'enthusiastic'?"

Davey came back in a short time. He had twelve cents change, which he offered to Skinny. "That's all right, keep the change," Skinny said grandly. "I'll take the full dollar—when you get one."

Davey reread both his letters, while Skinny made horrid noises on a clarinet which he had acquired during the summer.

After a while Skinny said, "Well, now that you've done me out of a dollar and five cents with that nose of yours, maybe you'd oblige with the dinner menu."

Davey went to the window and breathed deeply.

"Chicken soup," he sighed. "Irish stew, with dumplings, pickled beets—and rice pudding."